CICADA SUMMER

ANDREA BEATY

J
BEA

AMULET BOOKS

NEW YORK

Library of Congress Cataloging-in-Publication Data:

Beaty, Andrea.
Cicada summer / by Andrea Beaty.
p. cm.
Summary: Twelve-year-old Lily mourns her brother, and has not spoken since the accident she feels she could have prevented. The summer Tinny comes to town, she is the only one who realizes Lily's secret.
ISBN-13: 978-0-8109-9472-0 (hardcover)
ISBN-10: 0-8109-9472-0 (hardcover)
[1. Brothers and sisters—Fiction. 2. Emotional problems—Fiction. 3. Death—Fiction. 4. Grief—Fiction. 5. Secrets—Fiction. 6. Illinois—Fiction.] I. Title.
PZ7.B380547Ci 2008
[Fic]—dc22
2007022266

Text copyright © 2008 Andrea Beaty
Book design by Chad W. Beckerman

Printed and bound in U.S.A.
10 9 8 7 6 5 4 3 2 1

HNA ■■■■■
harry n. abrams, inc.
a subsidiary of La Martinière Groupe
115 West 18th Street
New York, NY 10011
www.hnabooks.com

MYRNA'S BOOK
—A.B.

1

THE CICADAS

SOME PEOPLE THINK THE CICADAS bring trouble when they come to town. I don't think that's true. I think trouble finds its way without any help at all.

The cicadas are everywhere. They came back to Olena two days ago, after seventeen years of hiding in the ground and waiting. Waiting to climb into the sunlight. Waiting to climb the bushes and trees. Waiting to sing.

They waited so long. Then, thousands of them crawled out of the ground and up into the trees and bushes in just one night. Their song sounds like electricity buzzing on a power line, getting higher and higher and louder and louder until the air nearly explodes from the noise.

There are a hundred cicadas on the oak tree outside Mrs. Kirk's sixth-grade classroom. I stand at the window watching them buzz from branch to branch. Their bodies are thick and clumsy, and I wonder how they can fly at all with their thin, little wings.

Then I see the cicada on the bookshelf next to me. It stares at me with its black marble eyes, and I stare back. I'm so close, I could thump it off the shelf if I wanted.

I could, but I don't.

At first, no one else notices the cicada. The other kids are hunched over their spelling tests, ready to spell *entangled* or *fearful* or *mottled* or some other word.

This week's words are adjectives, but Mrs. Kirk picked the wrong ones. She should have chosen words like *sweaty* or *noisy* or *stifling*. *Stifling* would be a good word today. It's so hot, it feels like July and the buzzing of the cicadas squeezes into the room and pushes out the air until no one can breathe. It's *stifling*.

I stare at the cicada, but even without looking, I know what's going on behind me. In the front row, Judy Thomas is wound up like a tiger ready to pounce on the next spelling word. She presses her pencil so hard against the paper that the lead nearly breaks. When Mrs. Kirk says the next word, Judy will spell it as fast as she can in her perfect handwriting, and then look around to make sure she's the first to finish. Of course she will be. She always is.

In the back row, where the hopeless cases sit— where there's a desk with my name on it—Rose

Miner is cheating off Tommy Burkette. Mrs. Kirk knows they're doing it, but she's too hot and too tired to care. Besides, the only person in the whole world who spells worse than Rose is Tommy, so it doesn't make much difference anyway.

After a while, the cicada on the shelf starts buzzing and Rose screams like it's Godzilla or something and Ricky Fitzgerald stands up and yells, "It looks like the cicada that got my grandma!"

Ricky Fitzgerald has told the story about the cicada that got his grandmother about a hundred times in the last two days. He says the last time the cicadas came around, one flew into his grandma's hair and made her run crazy around the yard until Ricky's grandpa came out with the sheep shears and lopped off half her hair.

I've seen his grandma's hair. She has one of those beehive hairdos that's tall and round and really hard from all the hairspray she uses. I can see why a cicada would land there. A hair cave like that would be a great place to get out of the sun.

That's what I think, but Ricky says it attacked his grandma to suck out her brains and make her into a zombie.

Ricky Fitzgerald is a dork.

Mrs. Kirk sighs the same way she has about ninety-nine times since the cicadas showed up and Ricky started telling his story.

"Thank you, Ricky," she says.

But before Ricky can say another word, Mrs. Kirk says, "Bobby, would you get rid of it, please?"

I could reach up and touch the cicada without trying, but Mrs. Kirk doesn't ask me. Bobby Bowes gets up from his desk and walks right in front of me. He grabs the cicada in one hand and opens the window screen with the other. He tosses the insect outside, closes the window screen, and sits down again without a word. He doesn't say, "Move, Lily," or anything. He doesn't even notice me standing there.

He doesn't notice because I'm invisible.

Most people would say that's a lie. They'd say that I'm not invisible because they can see me as plain as day. Most people are wrong. It's not my skin that makes me invisible. It's my silence. My silence and the trick I do with my eyes where I never look anybody in the face.

You can tell everything about a person by looking in their eyes. I don't want anybody to know anything about me, so I look away.

I've been invisible for two years now.

At first, everyone tried so hard to make me talk. They talked really loud to me and grabbed my face with their hands so I had to look at them, but I just shifted my eyes away and looked at the floor or the ceiling or something else. Anything else.

Almost everybody got tired of talking to me

after a while. That's when I faded away. They can still see me, but I'm like an old table to them. Just something to step around. Something to keep from knocking over.

Everyone gave up on me after a while. Everyone but Dad, who can't. And Fern, who won't.

It's been two years, and it's getting hard to remember when I wasn't invisible. Sometimes I wonder if I'll fade so much that I won't even be able to see myself.

After Bobby gets rid of the cicada, Mrs. Kirk goes on with the spelling test, but I don't stick around. I walk past Judy the Spelling Tiger and past the rows of kids scribbling wildly on their papers and out of the room. I walk down the hall with adjectives trailing behind me until I can't hear them anymore.

. . . speckled . . . tangled . . . futile . . .

I go into the school library and let Mrs. Todd's fan blow hot air over me while I stare at the Nancy Drew books. I never let anyone see me read one, and no one thinks I can anymore. But of course I can. I can do everything I used to do, but I don't let anybody know it.

I've read all of the Nancy Drew books at least fourteen times—except *The Haunted Showboat.* Some low-life book-thief stole that one. Book-thieves are the lowest form of criminal. I would never steal a book, but I put them in protective custody sometimes, and take them home and read them late at night when no one will see me. Of course I bring them back to school the next day.

If I think a book is really in danger, I hide it and keep it safe until I'm done reading it. I hide it in the gap behind the *Encyclopaedia Britannica*s that runs all the way from ORS to VEN. It's the perfect place to hide a Nancy Drew mystery. Or a Hardy Boys mystery, but who likes them?

Even with Mrs. Todd's fan, it's too hot to be in school, so I leave. I grab *The Clue in the Old Album* from the shelf and stuff it under my shirt and walk down the hall. Nobody says a word to me as I go. Nobody even notices the twelve-year-old girl walking out the front door of the school in the middle of the day.

I walk to the cottonwood tree at the edge of the school property. Out in the shade, there's nobody to get freaked out by the "brain-damaged girl" who can suddenly read.

I can just imagine what would happen if someone saw me.

"It's a miracle!" they'd say.

A miracle.

The cottonwood is enormous, and it stretches its branches like arms in every direction and dips its roots into Swift's Creek, which is a pretty funny name because there's no water in it. It's not swift. It's not even a creek.

I sink into the V between the giant roots and pull out my book and start to read. A cicada lands on my shoe and I let it rest there for a second before it flies off to look for its true love in another tree.

Dad says that the cicadas are so loud because they are looking for love. Every one of them is trying to sing the song that will attract the perfect mate, but it's hard to do when everyone else is so loud.

Dad tells me stuff like that at dinner when it's just the two of us alone together. He talks without waiting for an answer because he knows there won't be one. He talks because if he doesn't, the silence will eat him alive.

And all the time when he talks, his left hand is at his side, patting the hip pocket of his overalls like he's done a thousand times since he got up in the morning. His hand brushes the denim so lightly he doesn't even know he's doing it, but the denim is softer and lighter from his touch, and there are places where the threads are frayed from the hard edges and points of the keys in his pocket. He touches his pocket a thousand times a day to make sure he hasn't lost those keys.

When we are alone together, Dad talks about everything. About nothing. He talks because he can't stand the way I stare at my food. At the floor. At anything but him. Then, after a while, he stops talking and looks too hard at his grilled cheese sandwich and stirs his Campbell's tomato soup more than he needs to, scraping his spoon along the bottom of his bowl with hard, even strokes like the world depends upon it. I don't know. Maybe it does.

It's the hardest when I'm with Dad.

Hardest to stay invisible. I want to tell him all kinds of things. Small things, like about Ricky Fitzgerald's story and how someone stole *The Haunted Showboat*. I want to, but I can't.

If I start talking to Dad, I won't ever stop until it's too late.

Until I've told him everything.

Until I've told him about Pete.

Then Dad won't ever love me again.

How could he?

Pete and I stand at the edge of the road waiting to start our race to Fern's barn. We are racing for the Olympic gold medal, and I'm going to win.

Pete cups his hands around his mouth and calls out, "Racing for the United States of America in the three-thousand-meter dash is the reigning gold medalist, Pete Mathis."

He raises both arms up into the air and waves at

the cheering crowd. Then he cups his hands again and announces, "Racing for the Republic of Dorkonia is the World Champion Dork, Lily Mathis. Booooooooo."

I stick my tongue out at Pete, but I'm not going to waste my energy getting mad. It's time to race.

Pete narrows his eyes and grinds his back foot hard into the dirt. He gets down low, but I don't get so low. He says it's because I'm a girl and I don't really know how to run. I know it's because I'm scouting out the best way through the cornrows. He's trying to make me mad so I'll lose. But it won't work.

It never does.

"Racers, take your mark!" he says. "Ready . . . Set . . ."

And Pete takes off running and leaves me ten feet behind before he yells, "GO!"

Pete is such a cheater, but he has to be if he wants to beat me. I'm two years younger than him, but I'm almost as tall and I'm a lot faster than he is. I'm a lot like Dad that way. He's a good runner, too.

Dad says that Pete is more like Mom with his coal-black hair and green eyes, and the way they could both laugh and make you laugh, too—even when there's nothing funny to laugh at. I don't know if that's true. I don't remember Mom. Pete says he remembers her with purple flowers from the garden. It must be true because I've never seen purple flowers in the garden.

I race after Pete between two rows of corn that are almost up to my knees. The leaves scratch my legs a little, but I don't pay any attention. I'm catching up.

When Pete sees me out of the corner of his eye, he jumps out of his cornrow and into mine to stop me from passing, but it doesn't work. I know he's going to do it, so I jump into his row and run right past him. I stick my tongue out at him as I go.

I'm almost to the barn when a corn stob sails over my shoulder and lands right in front of me with a thud and a cloud of dust. I turn around and see Pete ready to bomb me with another one.

There aren't many stobs left in the field after this season's plowing and planting, but I find a good one and pull it out of the ground. It has about eight inches of dried cornstalk left and a big wad of roots and dirt stuck to the bottom, and it sails through the air like a missile right at Pete's head.

He ducks and then he gets up and throws another one at me really hard, and while I'm ducked down, he runs for the barn.

I get up and run as fast as I can, and we both hit the barn door at the same time and both of us are laughing so hard, that we can't either of us call the other one "loser."

Pete reaches into his overalls pocket and pulls out keys tied together with baling twine. He took them from the hook in the kitchen when Dad wasn't looking. Pete doesn't think Dad would mind, and he's probably right or Dad wouldn't leave the keys hanging around like that. Besides, we have to check that no gangsters are using the barn as a hideout. That's important. Fern wouldn't like gangsters hiding in her barn.

Pete unlocks the side door of Fern's barn and we step into the cool darkness. It still smells like hay, even though Fern hasn't had horses for years.

There isn't much in the barn. Just a dead plough, some busted crates, and two old cars. They belonged to Fern's husband who died a long time ago.

Mr. Fern loved his cars and always took good care of them. He kept them covered up and out of the rain. Fern loved Mr. Fern, so she keeps his cars covered up, too. Fern doesn't even know how to drive.

I go to the red sports car and pull back the cover. Nancy Drew's car was blue, but I like to think it was just like this one. It's a fancy car and I think maybe Nancy was a little bit spoiled.

And lucky.

Pete likes Mr. Fern's black sedan best because it reminds him of all the 1940s gangster movies he watches late at night on Channel 11. He loves those shadowy gray movies with tough guys and fast cars.

Pete pulls the canvas tarp back and bunches it up on the trunk. Dust flies into the air and gets caught in the shaft of light coming down from the hayloft window.

I love the way each speck of dust dances through the light, and then disappears in the shadows.

Pete opens the door of the sedan and slides behind the wheel.

"Hop in, toots!" he says. "I'll take you for a spin."

More than anything in the world, my brother Pete wants to drive.

"C'mon, toots!" he says again and he winks at me.

I jump into the convertible, which is right behind Pete's sedan. I see Pete's eyes narrow in his rearview mirror as he squeezes the steering wheel.

"You'll never take me alive, copper!" he yells and he makes a squealing sound like tires make on a hot road.

"You can't get away from the law, Bugsy!" I yell

back. The chase is on. We race through the countryside all the way to Chicago, where there are lots of other gangsters with fast cars. Pete grabs the stick he always keeps in the front seat. He shoots over the backseat at me. He makes a really good tommy gun sound, too.

"Eh–eh–eh–eh–eh!"

After a while, I get kind of bored and I yell, "You win this time, Bugsy, but I'll get you next time! You can't run away from the law!"

He yells, "See ya around, sucker!"

After that, I twist and turn the heavy steering wheel and I head down an old road that will lead me to a Haunted Showboat or the Inn of the Twisted Candle with my chums, Bess and George. We drive along looking for mysteries to solve until I hear Dad's tractor pass by Fern's barn and it's time to go home.

2

THE GIRL WHO KNOWS MY SECRET

I'M READING IN THE SHADE UNDER the cottonwood tree when Nancy Drew finds a big clue that's going to help her solve the mystery. It's a secret message stitched right into the design of a quilt. It's as big as day staring Nancy right in the face, and she doesn't even see it. I guess that's the best kind of clue— the kind you can't see right in front of your eyes.

I wonder if you have to be ready to see clues like that before they appear. Or maybe they have to be ready for you to find them.

I'm sitting in the shade trying to decide, when a long, flowery silk scarf dangles in front of my face and someone says, "I bet the butler did it."

It startles me so much that I break my number one rule of invisibility.

I react.

Before I can stop myself, I look up into the tree and straight into a pair of dark brown eyes on the face of a girl I've never seen before. She has a crooked smile and long black hair pulled back in a braid and she's wearing cutoff jeans and a blue shirt.

I'm trapped.

I grab my book and run. Behind me, I hear the cicadas stop for just a second while this girl laughs and swings out of the tree. I hear her yell something at me, and then the buzz of the cicadas swarms up and swallows her laughter.

Before the cicadas stop again, I'm gone.

I run all the way home and don't slow down until I get to Dad's zinnias by the front porch.

I guess Mom used to plant all the flowers, but now Dad does. He isn't very good at it, which is pretty funny because he's a farmer. Most of his flowers die or get eaten by rabbits, but the zinnias are tough and they always bloom. Red and pink and orange.

I'm glad something blooms for Dad.

I stop on the porch and look back at the field, but the girl is not following me. I go inside, past the rocking chair by the window. The green-and-orange afghan Fern crocheted is draped over the back.

Dad doesn't think I know how he stays up late sometimes, sitting by the window and watching Fern's barn, making sure I'm safe in the house. Sometimes he watches until he falls asleep in the rocking chair with the afghan pulled up to his shoulders.

He doesn't think I hear him as he climbs up the stairs at dawn, just in time to change into his overalls and start another day.

He doesn't think I know, but I do.

I run up the stairs and down the hall, past Dad's room and past Pete's room, letting my hand slide over Pete's white door as I go by. I always do that, but I never go in. No one does.

When I get to my room, I shut the door and look out the window. I don't see the strange girl anywhere.

I can't see the school from here, but I can see the road that runs from the school to Fern's store and then to our farm.

I see Thomas Keegan's collie, Lady, lying in front of Fern's screen door. I know in a few minutes, Fern will come out and toss her some scraps from the deli counter to get her to move, and Lady will move—until she's hungry again.

Fern's store is small and old with creaky wooden floors and a soda chest where I go and scrape the frost off the insides when it's really hot out. I squish the frost into a ball and rub it on my forehead and it melts and drips down my face.

Fern lets me come to the store anytime I want, and she talks to me without getting all close up in my face. She always waits a bit after she asks me a question just in case I might answer. But I never do.

Sometimes I pick up her broom and sweep the floor, but I don't look at her when I do it. And sometimes she grabs me up in her wrinkly, old arms and hugs me tight and calls me a Poor Motherless Child. I want to hug her back, but I don't.

I just suck in the air that surrounds her and hold it inside me as long as I can. Her white hair smells sweet like the Fresca she drinks, and spicy like the barbecue at her deli counter. And on top of that, she smells a little like honeysuckle perfume.

The girl isn't in front of Fern's store or on the road. I sit down on my bed and stare out the window, but all I see are the dark brown eyes of the girl who knows my secret.

I know all the girls in Olena.

There are only three girls in my class who live in town: Judy the Spelling Tiger, Carla Morgan, and me. All the other girls my age live way out in the country and take the bus to school.

Olena is smaller than tiny. The sign at the edge of town says the population is 200, but I think that includes dogs and cats and horses, because I never counted more than 117 people. That was when the Ericksons had a family reunion and about 30 people came to town.

Olena only has two roads. There's the big one that everyone calls the Hard Road because it's paved like a highway. It runs east and west through town and actually goes someplace else. The other road that heads north and south into the countryside is blacktop, but only as far as Neal's Hill. After that, it gives up and turns into gravel, and when it's gone so far nobody cares anymore, it narrows down to a dirt lane between soybean fields.

Pete and I used to ride our bikes out there, looking for lost civilizations, but we never found any. The Burkettes live out that way, but it would be a stretch to call them civilized.

There are a few houses on the Blacktop, and that's where Judy lives. Her house is almost at the top of Neal's Hill, but not quite. It seems a shame to me, because if her house was on the very top, she could sit on her porch and see the whole world. I guess it's best for Judy that her house isn't up that far, though, because she gets scared of heights. She didn't even know it until the time Carla Morgan pushed her too high on the swing and Judy got so scared she tried to jump off—but she wouldn't let go of the chains first. She was holding on for dear life. Even after she hit the ground, it took three of us to get her hands off those chains.

Judy never swung much after that.

Folks from somewhere else think it's weird not to know you're afraid of heights. But how could she know? Except for Neal's Hill, we don't have a lot of tall things in Olena. The fields roll up and down a little, but we don't have any mountains or even a water tower.

Most everything in Olena is on the Hard Road. At one end, there's the Olena First Baptist Church. I guess the first settlers were hoping for more people, but we never got enough for a

Second Baptist Church. Just a few Methodists out in the country, but they don't bother anybody.

At the other end of town, there's Fern's General Store.

Between the church and Fern's, there's the school and some houses and the post office, which is the only building in town that has air-conditioning.

Carla Morgan lives next to the post office. In the summer, Carla has a lemonade stand, and when it's really hot outside I walk close by. But not too close. Carla doesn't see me except when business is slow or she's bored. Then she grabs me by the arm and puts a cup of lemonade in my hand. She doesn't let go until I drink it all and drop the paper cup on the ground. Then she pats me on the arm like I'm a six-year-old or something and she says, "Good Lily. That was good."

I hate the way she says it, but sometimes, I'm just thirsty.

It isn't even two o'clock in the afternoon now. Carla and Judy are still in school with all the girls who ride the bus.

I know all of them.

Who is the black-haired girl in the cottonwood tree?

What does she want?

3

THE SEDAN

I SIT ON THE BED A LONG TIME, thinking about the strange new girl. Finally, I get up and go to Fern's General Store.

Every afternoon, the old men of Olena come to Fern's to wait for the evening paper and tell the town's secrets. Sometimes there are a dozen of them dressed in their overalls and caps. When it's hot, they lean against the counter and gulp down bottles of cold Pepsi in front of Fern's big fan.

They know that Ben Tucker will drive up at 4:15, same as he does every day, and toss a stack of newspapers out of his truck. They know that Ben is never early, but they show up at 3:30 for the news, and so do I.

When I get to Fern's, I grab the broom and go to the canned food aisle. The aisle is always empty. It's the best place to stand and hear everything in the store, and I can look through the shelves of beans and corn and see what's going on, too. I think Nancy Drew would approve.

I'm invisible while I sweep and listen to them tell about Reverend Riley White and why he had to leave the church or how Cassie Burkette got the farm instead of her brother, Ted. I learn a lot at Fern's. The old men of Olena know all the news that matters.

I'm sweeping in the canned food aisle when Cyril Johnson comes in. Mr. Johnson comes to Fern's every day after he picks up his mail at the post office.

When he comes to town, he doesn't wear the same overalls he wears to work in his fields or to slop his hogs. He changes into his newest pair of overalls with creases pressed into the dark blue denim. I think they go with the creases pressed into his face by the sun. He comes to Fern's for the paper, and when he gets there, he stands by the deli counter and doesn't say anything. I think Cyril Johnson is the only person in Olena who really comes to Fern's to get the newspaper.

I'm surprised when he walks past the deli counter and goes to the cash register where Fern is counting coins.

"Is it true, Fern?" he asks. "Is she back?"

I hear Fern drop a handful of coins into the cash register and shut the drawer.

"Finally," Fern says. Her voice cracks a little when she says it.

"And that father of hers?"

"Who knows," says Fern.

Then I hear someone else and I bend down to get a look between the cans of peas and hominy corn. The strange girl is there on the other side of the shelf from me, sucking on a Tootsie Pop. She has her back to me. Her flowered scarf is threaded through the belt loops of her cutoff jeans and she stands there with her hands sticking deep down in her pockets. She's so close I could poke her with the broom handle if I wanted to.

"Cyril," says Fern, "you remember my great-niece, Tinny? She's twelve, now. Can you believe that?"

"Oh my," he says quietly, "just look at you. Your mama and my girl Emma were like twins, you know. Couldn't throw a rock at one without hitting the other. We all miss your mama, but we're glad to have you back."

Then Fern grabs Tinny up in her arms and starts crying, "She's the spitting image of her mama."

Fern squeezes Tinny tight and rocks her back and forth. Tinny doesn't hug Fern back. She stands there with her hands in her pockets while Fern squeezes her.

There must be something wrong with Tinny because a hug from Fern makes you feel safe and warm and makes you want to hug her back. Even if you're a sneaky person like Tinny.

Even if you're a sneaky person like me.

Fern sobs, "Oh, you Poor Motherless Child."

Her words hit me right in the chest. Those words are mine. How can she say them to Tinny?

They knock me backward and I hit my arm on a can of peas and tip it over. Fern doesn't notice and neither does Mr. Johnson, but Tinny does. She twists around in Fern's arms and looks straight at me and smiles with her mouth, but not her eyes.

Just then, Ben Tucker drives up and tosses a bundle of papers off his old red pickup truck.

Somebody carries the bundle to Fern's cash register and she cuts the string and hands papers out to the customers who've already paid for them. It's easy to slide out of Fern's with the old men crowded around making important comments about the headlines like they've already read the paper.

I drift out the front door and start walking home. My heart pounds in my chest and I want to run as fast as I can, but there are too many people around and one of them might see me. I can start running when I get to Fern's bottle house, where she stores the empty soda bottles until the Pepsi man can come pick them up. But when I get there, Tinny's waiting for me.

She leans against the bottle house like she's really cool or something. Like she didn't run to get there first. She pulls the Tootsie Pop out of her mouth and rolls the stick between her fingers so the candy ball twirls.

"Well, well," she says. "You're a regular Nancy Drew snooping around, aren't you?"

I dodge her and keep walking, but she pushes her way in front of me and I have to stop. I lower my eyes and stare at a rock by her feet and wish I was somewhere else.

"Fern told me all about you. She says you're *special*," Tinny says. Her voice is drippy and sweet like a melted Popsicle. It makes me want to puke.

"I wonder if Fern knows how *special* you are . . ." she says.

I try to dodge her again, but she grabs my arm and twists me around so we're face to face. This time, I look her right in the eye. I give her a look that would melt iron.

"I could tell her," Tinny says.

Then she gives me this sly kind of smile and says, "Or maybe *you* could."

I try to jerk my arm free, but when I do, my hand scrapes against the neck of Tinny's shirt and pulls it to her left shoulder. It's like Tinny's struck by lightning. She drops my arm and jerks her top back into place, but not before I see the scar. It's the size of a quarter and it's white and puffy like it hasn't healed up yet.

Tinny straightens her shoulders and sticks her nose up in the air like she's royalty or something. Then she gives me that sly, crooked smile again and says, "Ain't you never seen a shark bite before?"

Tinny twists around on her heels and walks away like she's the Queen of Siam.

It hasn't rained for two weeks and the dirt lane to Fern's barn is finally dry. Dad gets the keys from the hook in the kitchen and climbs into the pickup truck. Pete and I hop in the back and sit on the round humps of the wheel wells and off we go.

It's a quarter-mile ride down the dirt tracks that circle around to Fern's barn. It's faster to run through the cornrows from our house to the barn, but we like riding in the back of the truck. When we get to the barn, Dad takes off the padlocks and Pete and I help him pull back the enormous red doors. Then we pull the sedan's canvas cover all the way off and fold it as neat as we can on the barn floor. While we work, Dad pops up the hood of the sedan to check the oil.

Dad goes to the barn every month to keep Mr. Fern's sedan running. He says the convertible is beyond hope, even though it's not as old as the sedan.

"It'd take a tow truck and a miracle to get that car rolling," he says.

The oil in the sedan is fine, so Dad drops the hood and starts her up and we head to town.

Fern is waiting for us when we pull up. She flips the sign in the store window to CLOSED and locks the door. She's wearing her best scarf and sweater, and the *hint of honeysuckle perfume mixes with old car smell as Fern climbs into the front seat.*

Dad honks the horn as we pass the school, and again when we pass the post office.

"Hello, you old school building!" Dad calls. "Hello, you old post office!"

We laugh and wave as we pass by. Then we drive into the country. The road rises and dips as it rolls between the fields and pastures. Dad honks at Cyril Johnson's cows as we pass, but they don't seem to notice.

Pete sits behind Fern so he can look over the seat and watch Dad drive. When Dad shifts, Pete copies his hand motion and presses his left foot hard into the floorboard like he's the one pushing on the clutch. Pete is teaching himself to drive just by watching.

Next year, Pete will turn thirteen and Dad will teach him to drive the truck down the dirt lane by Fern's barn. I think Pete will already know what to do by then. I think he already does.

Pete will drive the truck, but he really wants to drive Mr. Fern's sedan. It's what he wants most of all in the whole world, but it won't happen and Pete knows it.

We drive through the country, past tumbledown farmhouses where the orange lilies grow in clumps. Fern tells us about the women who used to live on those farms; the women who planted those lilies so long ago. I'm glad the lilies still bloom so people driving by remember those women.

And because I like the name.

After a few miles, Dad turns onto the gravel road that heads north and then curves back toward town. The gravel crunches beneath our tires and the dust flies up behind us as we drive along. Fern and Dad chat about this and that, but after a while, Fern gets quiet and closes her eyes, and her hand taps out the beat to a song only she can hear. And as I watch, the lines around her eyes seem to fade and even with her white hair, she looks young again.

Fern is not driving down a gravel road with Dad

and Pete and me. She's driving with Mr. Fern in his shiny new sedan on the way to nowhere in particular.

When the gravel road climbs up the backside of Neal's Hill and becomes the Blacktop, Dad slows down. He drives slower and slower until we reach the top and then he stops.

Nobody says a word as we sit at the very top of Neal's Hill and look at the whole world below us. The corn and bean fields spread like striped quilt patches in every direction. And straight down the hill, where the Blacktop meets the Hard Road is the X that marks the spot—Olena.

Fern sits perfectly still for a second with her eyes closed, and then she takes a deep breath and lets it out slowly.

Finally, she opens her eyes and smiles.

"I wonder if there's a store in that little town where a couple of kids could get some ice cream."

4

CLUES

I STAY AWAY FROM FERN'S FOR THE rest of the week. I don't go near the cottonwood either. I don't want to run into Tinny again, but more than that, I'm investigating.

Tinny is weird and I need to know more about her. I drift around the school and eavesdrop on everyone I can. I keep a list in my head of things I learn, and I write them down when I get home each day.

After four days, my list looks like this:

Clues

1. Tinny showed up at Fern's house with the clothes she was wearing and some money. Judy Thomas says it was $5, but Rose Miner says it was $2,576 and some change.

2. Tommy Burkette thinks Tinny is a Canadian spy.

3. Tommy Burkette is flunking 6th-grade Social Studies. Ignore number two.

4. Tinny's mom died five years ago. She was Fern's niece. That means that Fern is Tinny's great-aunt, which is almost as good as a grandma.

5. Tinny should be in 6th grade like me, but school's almost out, so Fern is letting her skip the rest of the year.

6. Tinny took the bus from Chicago to Walnut Grove and hitchhiked the rest of the way to Olena. Olena is 300 miles south of Chicago. That's a long way.

7. Ricky Fitzgerald thinks Tinny would make a good Catwoman. He's an authority, because he built a Bat Cave in his hayloft. He stole a pair of his mom's tights and her tablecloth and now he thinks he's a Caped Crusader.

8. Ricky Fitzgerald is a dork. Ignore number seven.

My whole list is dorky. Nancy Drew's prissy cousin, Bess, could do better and she's only in the Nancy Drew mysteries to make Nancy look good.

I have to find out more about Tinny. There's something bad about her and it makes me worry about Fern. I have to go back to the store, even if it means running into Tinny again.

Especially if it means running into Tinny.

On Saturday mornings, the farm women come to Olena to shop. And to talk.

Fern keeps a pot of hot coffee going, and the women bring in fresh-baked plum cake and cinnamon rolls and pie. Fern keeps a stack of paper plates and plastic forks on the counter. It's like a tea party with people coming and going, but there's coffee instead of tea.

The women bring stories, too. And secrets. Sometimes they're the same secrets the men tell, but sometimes they're different.

The women's stories are full of details, like who is related to who and where people live and what their houses are like. Their stories are all connected to each other and to the things that happened in the past.

Sometimes, when the store is crowded, there are four or five stories going at the same time, and the women's voices swirl around in the air and bubble up and splash like water on rocks. The sound is smooth and sweet.

If we had a real creek in Olena, I think it would sound like Fern's store on Saturday mornings.

I love Fern's store then, but I don't usually go. It's too hard to be invisible with the women of Olena. Some of them ignore me, but there are too many who don't. Almost all of them are mothers and they all want to help the pathetic girl who sweeps the floors.

That's what normally happens, but when I go to Fern's Saturday, no one even notices me. No one notices me because there's a new motherless girl to help.

Tinny is there with her long silk scarf wrapped around in her hair like a bandanna and she has on a new blue shirt that Fern bought her.

I notice that she has it buttoned all the way to the top.

The women fuss over Tinny like she's a baby

chick or something, and Tinny lets them, but I notice she doesn't answer when they ask her about Chicago or her father.

Tinny doesn't look at me, but she knows I'm there. I watch her from behind the cans of corn. I can tell that Tinny's always on the lookout, but she's sly about it.

She gets a good look at everyone who comes in, but she doesn't do it by staring. Tinny steals little glances when she doesn't think anybody will notice.

But I do.

And another thing: Tinny never lets anybody sneak up on her. She always stands with her back to the wall—and where she can run away if she needs to. When she gets blocked in by a couple of women, Tinny finds an excuse to go stand somewhere else.

Tinny is smart, but so am I.

I watch her standing with her hands deep in

her pockets, and when she pulls them out, I see something fall to the floor. Something she doesn't even notice. When Tinny moves to a new spot, I sweep where she was standing and find a red, square piece of paper folded into a tiny cube. I sweep it into my hideout behind the corn and unfold it. It's a Tootsie Pop wrapper and she has half-written, half-scratched something in pencil onto the waxy paper: PO309.

What does that mean?

Around eleven o'clock, the store starts to clear out. The women go back to their farms to make lunch for their husbands. I'm about to sneak out when Tinny moves close to the door and won't budge. She says "Goodbye" to all the ladies who leave like she's the hostess of a party or something. Fern goes to the deli case to make some sandwiches for the folks who will come in for lunch.

I try to slip out behind the last group of ladies to leave, but it doesn't work. When I reach for the screen door, Tinny grabs my arm and pulls me back. Then she uses that melted Popsicle voice, real loud so Fern can hear her all the way back to the deli counter: *"Oh, Lily!"* she says. *"Won't you stay a while and keep me company? It would be ever so nice."*

I try to tug my arm loose, but she has a tight grip. Tinny pulls me back to the cash register and leans against a shelf by the candy bars. Fern keeps the candy by the register so the Burkette boys won't steal it.

I stare at the floor and hope someone will come in so I can escape, but no one does.

"What's new, Lily?" Tinny whispers. "Read any good books lately?"

My heart beats hard and my cheeks get hot. Tinny looks over the rack of candy bars and taps each one once like she's counting them all. She half-sings to herself the same words over and over, "Choices, choices . . . my, oh, my . . ."

Then Tinny does something I can't believe.

She stops singing and grabs a Zero candy bar off the shelf and rips it open. She takes a big bite and grins while she chews so I can see the white nougat in her mouth.

Tinny is stealing from Fern.

In three bites, the candy bar is gone and Tinny crumples up the wrapper and jams it into her pocket.

I clench my fists and glare at Tinny's, and then she does something even more horrible.

In her sickening sweet voice, she says, *"Fern, is it okay for Lily to take candy?"*

I stand there like a deer in the road before a truck hits it, and Fern comes over.

Tinny smiles as innocent as a baby and she says,

"Lily is taking candy, so I wanted to make sure that's okay with you."

Then Tinny reaches into my shorts pocket and pulls out a Jawbreaker.

Tinny pulls a Jawbreaker out of MY EMPTY POCKET!

Fern does something amazing then. She grabs me up in her arms and squeezes me tight and says, "You Poor Motherless Child. You can have all the candy you want."

I want to hug Fern back more than ever, but I don't.

I twist around in her arms to look at Tinny. I think she'll be mad, but she just grins. She grins and holds her hand up behind Fern's head and pulls another Jawbreaker out of thin air like a dimestore magician.

She pops it into her mouth and grabs a Zagnut candy bar off the shelf and crams it into her pocket.

I can see that all of Tinny's pockets are lumpy when she walks out of Fern's store and lets the screen door slam shut behind her.

Tinny is trouble. She's up to no good and it makes me worry for Fern. Fern doesn't think Tinny can do anything wrong. She's just glad to have her around.

I need to look after Fern, so I go to the store every day. I go after school and stay until the paper gets there. Then I leave when the store is crowded.

Tinny hasn't bothered me again, but she's up to something.

Things are missing at the store. Things Fern doesn't even notice, but I do. When I sweep the floors and listen to the old men tell the town's secrets, I count all the things on the shelves.

I know every single thing in Fern's store. I know how many cans of corn are on the shelf; how many pairs of shoestrings are in the box. I know that Tinny steals lots of candy. But other things are gone, too.

Fern's store is missing four cans of tamales, eight bottles of Orange Crush, a package of toilet paper, and one copy of each magazine that came out in May. And some bug spray.

Fern keeps a list in the back of everything she sells. That makes it easy when she phones in orders to the Brewster Brothers Produce and Dry Goods Company. None of this stuff is on the list. Tinny has been busy.

But why?

Pete has been reading Tom Sawyer *and now he wants to go fishing. He thinks we should hike over to the Mississippi River since that would be authentic, but Dad says it's seventy-five miles to the river and Pete will have to find someplace else to fish—or a different book to read.*

Dad knows that the only place to fish in Olena is Johnson's Pond, since it's the only water anywhere around. They say there are catfish bigger than me in that pond, but nobody really knows.

Nobody fishes at Johnson's Pond without permission, and Cyril Johnson doesn't give anybody permission.

Cyril Johnson never says anything at all. He drives his green tractor to the post office every day just before four o'clock and people scoot out of his way. He walks up to the counter, gets his mail, and walks out without a single word. He just gets on his tractor and drives to Fern's for the paper.

Fern says that Cyril Johnson doesn't care about much these days but fishing.

That's all Pete needs to know.

On Monday, we go to the post office before Mr. Johnson shows up. Pete brings a fishing lure and shows it to Harold, the postmaster. When Mr. Johnson walks in, Pete is telling Harold all about the Canadian fishing trip he's going to take with Dad. Pete goes on and on about how much the trip means to him and how many years they've been saving just for the bait.

Mr. Johnson gets his mail and leaves. Maybe he knows a fish story when he hears one.

On Tuesday and Wednesday, Pete brings in his tackle box and he adds a remote lake and a seaplane to the story. Mr. Johnson doesn't say a word, but I notice he walks a little slower getting out of the post office.

While Pete's telling his stories, I put my time to good use. I read the black-and-white posters of the FBI's most wanted criminals. I study their pictures and try to memorize their scars and their eyes so I'll be ready. Just in case I ever meet one.

You can tell everything by a person's eyes. A person can change their hair and lose weight, but their eyes are always the same.

Except for Pete.

Pete could grow up to be a criminal. His eyes change color with the sky. Sometimes they're gray and sometimes they're green. That would confuse a witness.

And besides, Pete's smart enough to be a criminal. Some people think criminals are dumb and common, but the good ones are really, really smart. Pete's that smart. And he never blabs a secret. That's important for a good criminal. Jails are full of dummies who can't keep their mouths shut.

I'm a detective, and I might even have a hard time catching Pete if he became a criminal.

On Thursday, Pete takes his fishing reel and tackle box to the post office and he even wears Dad's old fishing hat. He looks like a real fisherman and I notice that Mr. Johnson stands inside the post office and sifts through his letters a long time before he finally leaves. He's never done that before.

Pete has hooked Mr. Johnson. Now he just has to reel him in.

Pete is a mastermind. I think he'll show up on Friday with a fishing boat just to prove he's really a fisherman, but he doesn't.

On Friday, Pete leaves everything but his fishing reel at home. He dresses in his rattiest overalls and his tennis shoes with the biggest holes in them. We wait until Mr. Johnson is inside before we go into the post office and when we do, Pete walks in with his head so low his chin nearly scrapes the floor. He looks like someone just ran over his dog and then backed over it to make sure it was dead.

Pete drags himself over to the counter where Mr. Johnson is standing and he says, "Harold, do you know anybody who would like to buy a fishing reel?"

Then Pete makes his eyes well up and I think he's going to start crying right there! He tells Harold how the crops don't look so good this year so Dad has to take the bait money and use it for seed corn.

"Maybe we can go when I'm all grown up . . . ,"

Pete says and he smiles the weakest, most pathetic smile ever, ". . . if Dad's not too old by then."

Then Pete heads for the door, but before he can turn the knob, Mr. Johnson clears his throat and says, "Oh, brother. You can fish in my pond already. Just watch out for snakes."

Cyril Johnson pushes past Pete and heads out the door. I'm not sure, but I think he's smiling.

Pete and I go fishing at Johnson's Pond three times and we catch a few tiny bluegills, but we never see any fish as big as me—just some mud turtles on a log and a snake's skin floating near the cattails.

I think Pete will want to keep fishing until we catch one of those monsters, but he doesn't. Pete has finished Tom Sawyer and started some new book. Pete says that fishing is boring.

Pirates are exciting.

5

OLD LADY PARTY

IT'S SIX O'CLOCK ON FRIDAY. TIME FOR an Old Lady Party.

Every Friday night, Fern and Miss Opal Page and her sister, Miss Pearl Page, come to our house for dinner, though they really come to our house *with* dinner.

Fern's not an old lady. She's just white-headed and wrinkly and has been around a long, long time. But the Page sisters *are* old. Nobody in Olena, or probably the whole state, is any older than Miss Pearl or Miss Opal. There used to be another sister named Sapphire, but she's been gone a long time.

The Page sisters are old, but they're still the best cooks in town. At least Miss Pearl is. Miss Opal likes to substitute ingredients and uses anything she finds close to the stove in her cooking. I always take a tiny taste before I dive into any of her dishes.

Our Old Lady Parties started when I was about six, because Fern noticed how much tomato soup Dad was buying in the store.

"Those kids will turn into tomato soup if you don't learn to cook, Paul Mathis!" she said.

That Friday night, Fern turned up on our porch with a pot of chicken and dumplings and a blackberry cobbler.

We let her right in.

The next Friday night, Miss Opal and Miss Pearl turned up with chocolate cake and fried chicken. We let them right in, too!

After that, all three of them started showing up every Friday night, and it was always a real party at our house. They brought enough food for us to eat until Tuesday.

Of course, Lottie Duncan felt like they were showing her up, so she started dropping by with food, too. She brought zucchini bread and some kind of "surprise salad" that had marshmallows and beans. And she stayed and stayed and talked and talked about how important it is to help the needy.

I don't think that sat too well with Dad, and I know the beans and marshmallow surprise didn't sit too well with Pete. Especially not the beans . . .

Some surprise.

Lucky for us, a tornado touched down over by Camel's Corner. It knocked over some telephone poles and scared some cows. Lottie figured the folks in Camel's Corner were needier than us, and she took them her next batch of surprise salad. I'll bet they were surprised, too. I was glad that Lottie found someone new to help, and I don't think Dad minded, either.

The food is great at our Old Lady Parties, even though I like Dad's food plenty, too. Dad can make grilled cheese and hotdogs and he can fry bacon and eggs pretty good. And in the summer, he makes bacon-and-tomato sandwiches and boils up corn on the cob straight out of the field. Nothing's better than that.

Still, it's nice to have a change now and then.

Dad loves our Old Lady Parties. When the old ladies get talking, their voices swirl like music around the room and Dad relaxes. He laughs like he used to with Pete and me, and he hardly ever touches his overalls pocket or stares too hard at his food.

I sit at the table between the Page sisters and listen to their music and I just breathe it all in. And they let me.

It's six o'clock on Friday and I'm at the kitchen table when Dad drives up with the ladies and helps them into the house, each carrying a dish of food covered with tinfoil. Even before they reach the hallway, the smell of roast beef and the music of their voices fill the kitchen and I breathe in deep until a voice like a melted Popsicle ruins everything.

"Why, just look, Fern!" the voice drips. *"Lily's here. I was hoping we'd see her again."*

While Fern and the old ladies bustle around the kitchen organizing the food they've brought, Tinny asks where the bathroom is.

"Upstairs at the end of the hall," Dad tells her. "You can't miss it."

Tinny's gone a long time. I'm starting to get antsy when she shows up again.

"You have such a beautiful home, Mr. Mathis," she says in her drippy, sweet voice.

Tinny is such a phony. I'd trust Al Capone before I'd trust her. I wonder how many bars of soap she has stuffed in her pockets. If I'd known she was coming, I'd have counted our soap.

When everyone sits down to the table, I'm between Miss Opal and Miss Pearl. Tinny sits across from me so she can watch me while I eat. Watch for me to mess up or give something away.

I stare at my food and eat slowly, but I hardly taste the roast for the bitterness in my mouth.

Tinny chatters on and on about how she just loves it here in Olena and what a big change it is from Chicago where it's so noisy and there are so many people everywhere.

Dad loves to hear about Chicago and asks Tinny lots of questions. He says he went there with Mom before they had Pete.

I never knew that.

Dad asks about all the places he and Mom visited to see if they are still there.

"Do they still have that big museum on the lake with all those dead, stuffed animals? And those masks from Africa?" he asks. "And mummies—do they still have mummies?"

Dad loves talking to Tinny. I can tell from his voice. He's happy and he can hardly wait to hear Tinny's answer to ask another question. It's like Dad is on vacation. He's so far from our farm. So far from me.

Tinny goes on and on about that museum. The Field Museum she calls it. It's one of her favorite places. But the place she misses the most is the Chicago Public Library.

"Chicago has the best library in the world," Tinny says. "I bet they have a million books in there, and you can take all of them out if you want. You just have to do it five at a time."

Then Tinny pauses and sips her iced tea and I know she's building up to something. And then she pulls out that Popsicle voice again and says, *"I bet Lily would love it."*

Those six words grab Dad by his heart and jerk him right back to the farm. Right back to me. He stops talking then and stares too hard at his dinner and he grabs his knife and cuts into his roast like the world depends upon it.

The only sound in the kitchen is Dad's knife scraping over his plate.

Fern jumps up and starts clearing the dishes from the table, but she stops when Miss Opal says, "No, she wouldn't."

"Who wouldn't what?" asks Miss Pearl.

"Miss Lily wouldn't like Chicago at all," says Miss Opal. "She tells me that all the time."

Dad drops his knife and Miss Pearl gasps.

"Why, Opal May, that's just not so," she says,

"and you know it. Miss Lily never said any such thing."

"Not out loud," Miss Opal says, "but she knows what she means."

Fern changes the subject as fast as she can.

"Just look here," she says. "Miss Opal made a cake!"

"It's apple cake," says Miss Opal. "I didn't have any apples so I used radishes. I asked Sapphy and she thought they'd work just fine—being red and all."

Miss Pearl slaps her palm on the table hard and stands up.

"Oh, for goodness' sakes, Opal," Miss Pearl says and she is mad when she says it. Then she turns to Tinny and she says in a voice that's calm, but you can tell it's only calm on the top, "Please excuse my sister, Miss Tinny. She sometimes forgets our sister, Sapphy, is gone."

Then Miss Opal says in a voice that is calm

through to her very soul, "Please excuse *my* sister, Miss Tinny. She always needs to see a thing with her eyes or hear it with her ears to believe it."

Then Miss Opal leans close to me until our shoulders touch and she turns and whispers so only I can hear, "That's why she misses so much."

And Miss Opal May Page reaches under the table with her cool, wrinkled old hand and grabs my hand and she squeezes it. And because I know nobody else will see and even more because my heart swells up in my chest and might bust if I don't do something, I squeeze back.

We've been working on our pirate ships for a week. Tomorrow we'll sail them in Johnson's Pond. At least that's the plan, but near midnight Pete sneaks into my room and wakes me up.

"Ahoy!" he whispers. "The Red Dragon sails at midnight!"

And then Pete is gone. I get out of bed and put on my clothes and sneak down the stairs. The front door is open, so I know Pete is outside, but I can't see him anywhere even though there's almost a full moon. It doesn't matter, because I know exactly where he's going.

When I reach the Hard Road, I start running toward town. I can't see far down the road, but after a minute, I make out a shadow ahead. It's Pete carrying his fishing reel and the cardboard box that holds our pie-plate ships.

He's moving fast, but I'm faster and I catch up to him and grab him by the elbow.

"Stop," I whisper. "What are you doing?"

"Having a pirate battle," he says. "It's more authentic at night."

"We have to go home," I say. "Dad'll find out!"

"Not unless you tell him," Pete says and he jerks his arm free and starts down the road again.

I stand there watching him walk away in the dark.

"Stop!" I whisper as loud as I can, but Pete doesn't stop. He keeps walking, his shadow getting fainter and fainter as he goes.

I look back at our farm. It's so far away. So quiet.

I turn back toward Pete. I can barely see him now, a dark motion in the night, almost gone.

I stand there just a second, but it feels like forever. I look again at the farm and then back to Pete, but even his shadow is gone now.

And then I run. I catch up to Pete near Fern's store.

"What if Dad wakes up?" I whisper.

"Dad doesn't like pirates," he whispers back.

And that's all we say as we cross town in the dark and head to Johnson's Pond.

The pond sits in a pasture fenced off by barbed wire. Pete squeezes under the fence and I hand him the ships and fishing reel. Then I squeeze under, too.

The pasture grass is tall, but I'm in jeans so I don't mind. As we push through the tall grass on the way to the pond, I try not to think about Mr. Johnson's warning in the post office: Watch out for snakes.

When we reach the pond, we set the ships at the edge of the water. There are four of them—three flying the Union Jack and one the Jolly Roger. Each ship has a mound of clay in the bottom that holds up a mast made of sparklers lashed together with thread. The sails are cut from an old bedsheet. Pete found a new can of motor oil in the garage and we soaked the sails in the thick, golden oil for a week.

The pirate ship is armed with an extra-long sparkler that juts out the front like a unicorn horn. Pete says that's called a "bowsprit," and I should know that if I'm going to be nautical.

Pete likes knowing the names of things. Pete likes being authentic.

He hooks the pirate ship to the line of his fishing reel. Then he pulls a bundle of extra sparklers from his overalls pocket and fishes out a book of matches, too.

One by one, I shove the English ships gently from the shore. They twirl in lazy circles toward the center of the pond.

"Avast!" Black Pete cries. "Thar be gold in them ships! Set sail the Red Dragon!"

Black Pete takes up the fishing pole and walks around the edge of the pond letting out line as he goes. When he gets to the opposite shore, I light a match and hold it to the Red Dragon's bowsprit. The sparkler catches with a hiss and electric-white sparks shoot out in every direction and reflect off the black water. Then Black Pete reels in the line and the pirate ship sails straight and true toward the first British ship—the HMS Crackle.

The flaming bowsprit touches the HMS Crackle's mast and it erupts in sparks. The sparks climb the mast and touch the oil-soaked sails and they catch fire and burn with a bluish-yellow flame that glows across the whole sea.

"*Take the helm, Red Lily,*" Black Pete *calls, and I sail the* Red Dragon *to port to refit her with a new bowsprit. Then we hunt the HMS* Pop *and HMS* Snap *across the Sargasso Sea until none sail those waters but the* Red Dragon.

At last, we fit the Red Dragon *with our seven leftover sparklers and set her adrift. The sparklers burn white-hot and the sail catches fire and falls. In an instant, the* Red Dragon *lists and takes on water and sinks into the murky depths.*

Black Pete and I watch the Red Dragon *until all that is left of her is a thin film of oil rising to the surface of the water. The oil pulls in the moonlight and shimmers and swirls, inky and black and beautiful.*

Oil on midnight water.

6

THE DREAM

MISS PEARL CALLS FERN WITH HER grocery order on Monday afternoon while I'm sweeping near the door. The Page sisters don't drive, so they call Fern once a week and she delivers groceries to their house. Pete and I used to carry the bags down the block to their house, and Miss Pearl would give us each a silver dollar and sometimes brownies, too. I don't know which was better.

Fern writes the order on the back of a paper grocery bag and sends Tinny around to find eggs, baking powder, sliced American cheese, Oreo cookies, and three packets of Teaberry chewing gum. Miss Opal can't chew gum with her dentures, but she puts it in her pockets to make her clothes smell nice.

Fern calls out each item as she puts it in the bag.

". . . eggs . . . three packs of gum, and Oreos. That's it," she says and she hands the bag to Tinny.

Tinny pushes open the screen door and steps outside, but before she walks off, Fern turns to me and says, "Lily! Why don't you go with Tinny to see Miss Opal and Miss Pearl?"

And for the first time, Fern doesn't wait for me to answer before she goes on. "They would just love to see you," she says and she puts her arm around me and gives me a squeeze and walks me out the door right behind Tinny. Then Tinny grabs my hand and pulls me down the sidewalk.

I want to jerk my hand loose and run away, but

I know Fern is watching from the doorway because I haven't heard the screen door shut.

Tinny hums as we head down the street. We're almost at the Page sisters' house when she says, "You know, Lily, you're really quite interesting. I've heard so many stories about you."

I pull my hand free and turn to walk off, but then she says something that makes me freeze.

"It's so mysterious though," she says. "You know, about the barn and all. So many unanswered questions, wouldn't you say?"

I don't even look at her, but I know she's wearing her snotty, crooked grin when she says, "No, I guess you wouldn't."

I stand there as she walks up the steps to the Page sisters' house and rings the doorbell.

"Well," she calls back to me, "I'm sure I'll figure it out."

My heart bangs in my chest, and I want to

run a million miles away from Tinny, but the door opens and I hear Miss Pearl call out, "Oh, look, Opal! We have company!"

Miss Pearl and Miss Opal take us to the kitchen and give us brownies and milk. I don't touch my brownie, but Tinny eats hers in two bites and gulps down her milk. Then she reaches over and takes my brownie and eats it, too.

Miss Pearl sets the brown paper bag on the table and starts putting away the groceries. Each time Miss Pearl pulls out an item, Miss Opal says, "Oh, my. That Miss Fern picks out the best groceries."

She holds up an egg like she's admiring a diamond.

"Just look at this egg," she says. "That Miss Fern is the best egg picker ever!"

When Miss Pearl pulls out a bag of Oreo cookies, Miss Opal, says, "Orioles! Elves make those in a hollow tree, you know."

Miss Pearl says, "No, dear, those are the other brand of cookies. These are made in Ohio."

"I wish they'd employ local elves," Miss Opal says. "We have a perfectly good hollow tree in the backyard."

Miss Pearl doesn't say anything because a coughing fit hits and she has to leave the room, but she runs back into the kitchen when Miss Opal cries, "Pearl! There's something wrong with the groceries. Pearl! Come quick!"

Miss Opal turns the grocery bag upside down and shakes it hard and two packs of gum tumble onto the table. The bag is empty, but Miss Opal shakes it harder and harder trying to find the third pack of gum.

"Pearl!" she cries. "That's not right. Miss Fern *always* sends three packs. She knows I need three. That's not right, Pearl. That's just not right."

She says it over and over and shakes the bag

harder and harder until Miss Pearl gently takes it away from her and sets it on the floor.

"That's not right," Miss Opal says again and again and her voice gets shakier each time she says it until she's half sobbing and her voice is small and scared, but she can't stop saying it.

Then Miss Pearl puts her arms around Miss Opal and rocks her gently and whispers, "Shhhhhh. Don't worry, honey. We'll find the gum. Don't worry."

They stand that way a long time—Miss Pearl rocking Miss Opal until she is finally quiet.

Then Tinny walks over to Miss Opal and says, "I found the gum, Miss Opal. It was on the floor."

She says it, but I know it's not so. Tinny hands Miss Opal the pink pack of gum and Miss Opal takes it and squeezes it tight in her fist and lets out a long sigh.

"I knew Miss Fern would send it," she says. "I

knew she would. She always sends me three packs. I knew Miss Fern would send it."

"Yes, Opal," Miss Pearl says softly. She sounds relieved and a little bit tired. "That Miss Fern always picks out the best groceries."

Miss Pearl reaches into her pocket and pulls out two silver dollars, one for me and one for Tinny. She tucks one into my pocket and turns to give one to Tinny, but Tinny is already gone.

I start having this dream.

I dream of Pete. Of driving with him in Mr. Fern's sedan, past the old farms where the orange lilies grow.

Every night, I wake up with the sound of squealing tires and screeching metal and screams. I wake up and I'm sweaty and scared.

I don't want to sleep anymore because I know what will happen when I close my eyes. I do everything I can to stay awake. I read under my covers with the flashlight I took from the kitchen. I have three Nancy Drew books in protective custody now—and I need them all. I'll have to bring home more before school ends to get me through the summer. I wish I could find the thief who took *The Haunted Showboat.*

I read and read until my eyes are so tired everything gets blurry and nothing makes sense anymore. I read until I'm so sleepy I can't stay awake.

When I fall asleep, I'm so tired I don't think I'll ever wake up.

I'm so tired, I don't think even dreams can find me.

But they do.

Next week is Pete's birthday. He'll be twelve, but he wishes he was going to be thirteen.

On his thirteenth birthday, Dad is going to let Pete drive his green truck up and down the dirt lane to Fern's barn. Fern said it was okay with her.

If Pete is a good driver, Dad will let him drive the truck in the fields at harvest time and he might even let Pete help with the combine. It's okay for Pete to drive without a real license as long as he doesn't leave the farm.

It's a whole year until Pete can drive, but he thinks he's ready now. When Pete walks by Dad's pickup, he lets his hand brush along the green paint gently like he's petting a new calf. He doesn't think I see, but I do.

Pete wants to sneak over to the barn every day to get in Mr. Fern's cars. Last night, he came sneaking to my room way after midnight to get me to go with him to the barn.

I told Pete that sneaking into the barn during the day was one thing, but at night, it would be criminal trespass for sure, and besides, he was too ugly to hang his mug shot at the post office. Pete said I was a Goody Two-shoes Party Pooper, but he went back to bed anyhow.

Crime fighting might cause problems between me and Pete someday.

7

THE STRANGER

store when the stranger comes to town. He's tall and thin and he's dressed in a County Water District shirt.

I'm in front of the deli counter. Tinny is behind it, wiping down the glass on the meat case. She can't see the tall man, but when he speaks, she stops wiping.

He says that he's a surveyor and that he'll be in town for a few days to double-check some old water maps.

It's a nice story, but it's a lie.

I know it because of his shoes. I don't dare

look at people's faces when the store is crowded, but I know all their shoes.

This stranger's shoes have never been on a dirt road or in a cornfield or even on a blacktop road. They don't have dust or mud or tar on them. They're polished and expensive. City shoes.

I hear the soft click of the storeroom door and look behind the meat counter. Tinny's wet sponge is on the floor and she's gone.

The stranger pulls an Orange Crush out of the icebox and he walks back to the deli counter. He stands beside me, looking at the sandwiches in the deli case. He stands so close I can smell the cherry Life Saver he's sucking on, and I can hear him click it around on his teeth while he looks over the sandwiches.

His left arm hangs down by his side, and on his hand he wears a strange silver ring with a crescent moon cut from the band.

I want to duck into the storeroom with Tinny, but I can't move. I stand there frozen while he looks over the sandwiches in the deli case and half-sings the same words over and over.

"Choices, choices . . . my, oh, my . . ."

Tomorrow is Pete's birthday and he's nervous like a cat.

Pete can't decide what he wants to do. He doesn't want to race to Fern's barn or go fishing or anything.

When I sit beside him in the swing, he gets up and leans against the porch rail, not saying a single thing. When I ask him what's wrong, he goes in the house and slams the screen door behind him.

What's up with Pete?

It's Tuesday and the store is empty except for Fern and me and Tinny.

Fern and Tinny are whispering together by the deli counter. I hear Fern say, "No, she couldn't . . ." but she doesn't sound too sure.

Then Fern goes back to the storeroom where she keeps the phone and Tinny comes out and stands by me.

"You really did it this time," she whispers. I look up at her, square in the eye. She's smiling.

At first, I don't get what she means, but in just a minute, Dad comes in and marches right back to where Fern is and I hear her say, "Paul, it's Lily. I think she's been stealing from me. I know it's not like her, but she's been acting a little strange and I think maybe she's jealous of Tinny."

"She can't be, Fern," Dad says. "You know she can't be."

"Paul, it's okay," she says, "but I think maybe Lily should stay home for a while."

Dad comes out to where I am and grabs my hand.

"I'm sorry, Fern," he says. "I'm so—"

But his voice dries up to a whisper before he can finish the words.

I hate Tinny.

I want to burn a hole through Tinny with my eyes. I want to stare at her so hard she catches on fire. I want to, but it's my eyes that burn, and everything gets blurry so I stare at my shoes instead. I blink and a drop of water falls and leaves a spot where it hits the wooden floor. I slide the toe of my sneaker over the spot so no one sees it and I squeeze my eyes shut.

Dad grabs me by the hand and pulls me out of Fern's store, and when the screen door creaks and slams behind us, he lets go of my hand and walks toward the truck and even the buzz of a million cicadas can't fill the silence that he leaves behind him.

8

MIDNIGHT

PETE STAYS UP LATE TALKING WITH DAD at the kitchen table, but I don't want to hear more about driving, so I go up to bed.

I watch the blocks of light slide across my wall as cars pass by the house and their headlights sneak through my window. I watch those lights and wonder who is driving by so late at night. Where are they going and what are they up to?

I bet it's no good.

I imagine what would happen if a car stopped at our farm and a shadowy, sinister character of medium

build sneaked up my stairs looking for a missing locket or maybe an antique clock that I somehow got hold of. There'd probably be a map or a key inside, and they'd need it back to find some loot. They'd stop at nothing to get it.

The burglar would climb the stairs quieter than a cat and open my door and slip into my room. He'd be there to strangle me in my sleep and ransack my room until he found what he was looking for.

That's what he'd plan, but I'd have different plans. I'd spring out of bed and knock him unconscious with my tennis racket. I'd use my backhand, because it's my best stroke.

It's eleven o'clock before I hear Dad and Pete climb the stairs and go to their rooms. Before I fall asleep, I reach beneath my bed to make sure my tennis racket is handy.

Just in case.

It's midnight. I wake up when I hear the clock downstairs chime. I close my eyes again and then I hear it—a click and a thud somewhere in the house. In the kitchen, maybe.

I listen closer. Even the tree frogs and crickets outside must have heard the sound, because they stop creaking and listen, too.

Is someone in the house? Is it a thief? A murderer?

And then I get a thought I've never had before. What if there's more than one bad guy? I hadn't planned for that.

Even with a good backhand, a tennis racket won't stop two bad guys at the same time.

What should I do?

If I hide behind the door, I can swing at one guy, but the second one will get me. I could yell for Dad and Pete. But what if the bad guys are already in the hall? If I yell, Dad and Pete will run right into a trap.

The only thing to do is pretend to sleep. And wait.

If the bad guys come and look at me, they might leave if they think I'm asleep. Then I can jump out of bed and hit them one at a time. I might have a chance.

I grab my tennis racket to my chest and pull my covers up to my chin and wait with my eyes closed but not so tight that I look like I'm faking it. I breathe deeply and slowly, just like I would if I was really asleep.

I just hope they can't hear my heart pounding in my chest.

❧

I can't go back to Fern's.

After school every day, I roam around town. When I get too hot, I go into the post office where the air-conditioning pours over me like a stream of icy water. I want to read the wanted posters, but the post office is too busy. People take a long time getting their mail when it's so hot outside.

I walk out to the edge of the field and look at

Fern's barn, but I can't go there. I can't even walk into the field. I sit at the edge of the road and watch a line of ants carry off bits of a dead grasshopper.

I can't go anywhere else, so every day, I go to the cottonwood tree.

I always check the branches to make sure Tinny isn't hiding up there before I sit down in the V and read *The Hidden Staircase.*

That's where I am on Thursday when I hear voices. I don't have time to run away, so I stick my book behind me and pull my legs up into the V and get as small as I can.

I hear someone scuffling around, and something bangs up against the tree and I hear Tinny.

"Leave me alone," she says. She's out of breath and her voice is shaky.

"I don't think so," says a man. I recognize his voice from Fern's store. It's the man with the ring. His voice is soft, but it has a sharp edge to it.

"You're a hard person to find, Tinny," he says, "almost as hard as your father."

"What do you want?" Tinny asks.

"Let me see," he says. "What could I possibly want?"

Then his voice gets mean.

"I want to know where your daddy is, so why don't you tell me, like a nice little girl . . ." he says. "You're a nice little girl, aren't you, Tinny?"

"I don't know where he is," Tinny says. "I ain't seen him since he dumped me at the bus station in Chicago."

I hear the crackling of paper and Tinny says, "Look. I got a hundred bucks. I'll give it to you if you just go away."

"A hundred bucks?" he says and he laughs. "You think I'd come to this backwater pit for a lousy hundred bucks? Don't make me mad, Tinny. You remember what happens when I get mad, don't you?"

"Don't!" Tinny cries and then something happens. He pushes her or maybe she falls. When she hits the ground, she lands by my feet. The wad of money in her hand flies loose and dollar bills scatter over the roots of the cottonwood.

That's when Tinny sees me.

Her eyes are wild and she tries to scramble away from me, but it's too late. The Ring Man comes after Tinny and when he steps around the tree, he sees me, too. His face is red and the veins in his neck bulge out and he reaches down to grab my arm, but Tinny gets between us.

She pushes the Ring Man and he stumbles over a root and hits the ground. Then Tinny's up yanking me out of the V.

"Leave her alone!" she yells. "She don't know nothing. She don't even know how to talk."

The Ring Man gets up and comes at me, but Tinny gets between us again and she puffs herself up like she did by Fern's bottle house. Her voice is fierce and it makes the Ring Man stop.

"Take the money and get out of here, Jake," she says.

Then Tinny grabs me by the hand and says, "Come on, Lily. Fern's waiting for us."

I sneak a look at his eyes. They're cold and dark and mean. That one look tells me everything I need to know about the Ring Man.

Tinny leads me right past him. I think she'll let go of my hand and run when we get to the Hard Road, but she doesn't. She holds my hand and walks through town with her chin sticking high in the air like she's the Queen of Siam.

We're almost to Fern's store when the Ring Man drives up beside us in a long black car. Tinny doesn't stop walking. She pretends she doesn't notice him, but I know she does because she squeezes my hand a little tighter.

"You forgot something," the Ring Man says and he tosses my Nancy Drew book on the road. The book flies open and Tinny's money flutters out onto the pavement.

"Oh, yeah, Tinny," he says, "tell the old woman she makes great egg salad. I'll have to come back and get me some more of them sandwiches."

Then he squeals his tires and speeds off.

Tinny pushes my hand away and she turns on me.

"Go home, Lily," she says. "Fern don't want to see you no more. Neither do I."

She tries to sound mean when she says it.

But she just sounds scared.

9

PETE

I LISTEN AND LISTEN, BUT I DON'T HEAR another suspicious sound in the house. I'm about to fall asleep when I figure it out.

It wasn't bad guys in the house at all. It wasn't thieves or murderers. It was Pete and he was sneaking off to Fern's barn. I know it. It makes me so mad. He knows he's breaking the law. He's criminally trespassing for sure. Or worse.

I jump into my clothes and creep down the hall to Pete's room. Sure enough, his pillows are stuffed under his sheet like a body. The oldest trick in the book.

I sneak downstairs and onto the porch as quiet as a ghost. My sandals are there, but Pete's are gone.

The moon is full over Fern's barn in the middle of the field. I should go upstairs and tell Dad what Pete is doing, and I'm so angry I almost do it. But I know if I do, Dad will be even madder than me and he won't let Pete drive until he's a hundred. Then Pete will be madder than both of us.

Pete already thinks I'm a Goody Two-shoes Party Pooper. He'd never forgive me if I was a snitch, too.

I cross the road and start running as soon as my sandals hit the soft dirt between the cornrows. When I reach the barn, the side door is open so I slip inside. And when I do, I hear the rumble of the car engine.

The rumble seems so loud, I pull the door closed behind me to keep the noise inside—to keep it from drifting through the darkness to Dad and waking him up.

The moon shines through the hayloft window and

fills the barn with a grayish light and there is Pete sitting in the driver's seat of Mr. Fern's sedan with the biggest smile in the universe.

"Hop in, toots!" he says. "I'll take you for a spin."

"I'm going to tell Dad," I say.

"No you won't," Pete says, but he doesn't say it in a snotty way or a mean way. He says it like it's the simplest fact in the world. And I guess it is a simple fact, because I don't move. My face is hot and I feel like I'm going to explode if I don't do something, but I don't move at all.

Dad would be so mad if he knew, and he needs to know. I want to turn around and run out of the barn and tell him, but I just stand there and watch Pete behind the wheel of Mr. Fern's sedan.

And then Pete laughs. And it's just like Dad says about Pete and about Mom, how they could make you laugh when there's nothing to laugh about.

When Pete laughs, my anger gets all jumbled up inside me. I'm still mad. But now it's not the same mad I had a minute ago. Somehow I'm not mad at Pete for stealing Dad's keys and trespassing in the barn. I'm mad because he didn't ask me, too.

And I'm even madder at me because I know if he'd asked, I would have said no.

Then Pete winks at me like he knows what I'm thinking and it's none of it really that important.

"C'mon, toots," he says and he tilts his head toward the passenger seat and winks again. "It's okay."

And somehow it is. Pete sits there in Mr. Fern's sedan with the tarp pulled back to the trunk and the engine rumbling and somehow it's okay.

It's after midnight and it's his birthday. Pete is twelve and he has his wish. He's driving Mr. Fern's sedan, even if it doesn't move an inch.

I should yell at Pete. Make him shut off the motor and go home. I should run home and tell Dad what

Pete's doing. I should, but I don't. Without a word, I go to the red convertible and pull the cover back and climb into the driver's seat.

It's too dark to see the rearview mirror in the sedan, but I know Pete is looking in it and narrowing his eyes like he does when we're about to race. Then he pushes on the gas pedal and makes the engine growl louder and louder. He thinks he can beat me—lose me on the long road to Chicago—but Pete can't lose me. There's no place Pete can go where I can't follow.

Pete drives all the way to Chicago with me right behind him and then I chase him to San Francisco and New York and Paris, and Pete sings his song about the place in France where the ladies wear no pants, and then he wants to go to Mars where the men all drive new cars, but it's a long, long drive to Mars, and somewhere near Saturn I start to yawn and I close my eyes for just one second . . .

I dream of Saturn, and its rings are purple and red and gold.

I live on one of the rings, but somehow my ring is covered in cornfields and grass and it looks just like Olena.

Then I'm looking out a window and I see the insects.

Hundreds of insects. And they're big like bats but some of them are blue and red, and some are white. Their wings make a low rumble as they fly, and the sound gets louder and louder and louder as they swarm over their prey. They fly around the yard this way and that way, chasing someone I can't see.

"Stop!" I scream.

And then they see me. Like one big cloud, they lift off the body on the ground and turn toward my window. They buzz louder and louder and higher until the sound turns into a scream and they land on my window screen.

I should run, but I can't. I look into their black, marble eyes and they draw me nearer and nearer. I lean closer, until my face presses against the screen and their stingers pierce through the metal wires into my cheeks. It burns, and I scream. I slap at my face. Over and over and over . . .

When I wake up, I'm lying outside the barn at the edge of the field and Dad is leaning over me. Shaking me.

"Lily! Wake up!" he yells. "Oh, God, Lily! Wake up! Can you hear me, Lily?"

He slaps my cheeks, but he seems so far away, I can hardly feel the sting of it. It's so hard to keep my eyes open, but then I see the fire truck and the police lights, and I see the firemen all kneeling in a huddle over something on the ground.

I recognize Thomas Keegan. His fireman's hat is tossed onto the ground and his red hair catches the flashing of the red lights and looks like it's on fire.

I wonder if someone will squirt him with the hose, and I want to laugh, but the sound won't come out. It's too far away.

Thomas pushes up and down on something over and over, but I can't see what, so I watch him for a long time until I see Fern standing with Miss Opal in the dark. Miss Opal is crying, and Fern is staring at Thomas with this weird look on her face.

Then Fern looks at me and for a second I see her eyes. You can tell everything by looking in a person's eyes. Everything you really need to know.

I look into Fern's eyes and I know everything.

Thomas Keegan stands up at last and the firemen move away from the shape on the ground, and the flashing red-and-blue lights swarm into the darkness they leave behind and slide over the dark, limp body laying there. I see a shock of black hair tinged red then blue then red . . .

The color is deep and inky like oil on midnight water. I saw that once at Johnson's Pond with Pete . . .

. . . Pete . . .

Carbon monoxide poisoning.

I hear it in the whispers that swirl around me. The whispers of the doctors and the nurses and the visitors who come and stand over my hospital bed. They shake their heads while I look away and pretend I'm somewhere else. Somewhere far, far away.

"Poor Pete," the whispers say. "Fern found them."

"Maybe if there had been a window open . . .," the whispers say. ". . . Or a door."

A door.

"Brain damage. She hasn't said a word since the accident."

Words were all I needed to save Pete.

I could have told Dad what Pete was doing, but I didn't do it.

I didn't use my words to save Pete, so I won't ever use my words again.

I promise.

10

GONE

TINNY IS GONE.

I know it when I hear Fern in the front parlor with Dad.

It's Saturday afternoon and Fern should be in the store selling sandwiches, but she's downstairs crying instead.

I tiptoe halfway down the stairs to watch their reflection in the china cabinet across the hall. The reflection is wavy and dim, but I can see Fern and Dad. Cyril Johnson is there, too, twisting his farmer's cap in his hands.

"When did you see her last?" Dad asks.

"This morning when I left for the store," Fern says. "I came back this afternoon and she was gone. We've looked everywhere for her."

Dad presses his hand against his hip pocket and squeezes the keys through the faded denim of his overalls. Fern reaches over and touches his arm.

"We checked there first, Paul," she says. "Tinny's not there and the barn is locked up tight."

Fern holds up a letter.

"I found this in my post office box," she says. "I have the only key, so I don't know how she got that lock open. She's so clever."

Tinny is not clever. She's sneaky and she's a thief. I'd bet anything she picked the lock to Fern's post office box.

It makes me so mad the way Fern still thinks

she's wonderful. But then Fern starts to cry again, and I can tell her heart is breaking and it makes me feel tight and twisted down deep in my stomach.

Dad takes the letter and reads it out loud.

Dear Fern,

When you get this, I'll be gone. You're a nice lady, but I don't like this backwater pit, so I'm going back to Chicago. Don't try to find me or send the cops to bring me back. I'll run away again. I swear it.

Tinny

P.S. Lily didn't take the money. It was me. I'm sorry, but I'll pay it back when I get

a job. I'll pay interest, too, like
a loan.

P.S.S. Tell everybody where I
went.

After Dad reads the note, he gets quiet for a bit. Then he says, "We might catch her in Walnut Grove if she hitchhiked back to the bus station. We can check the other towns up the line, too. What do you think, Cyril?"

"She might have gone for the train over in Murphydale," Mr. Johnson says. "I can head over there and check. Why don't you and Fern see about the buses? One of us will find her."

Fern says, "What if something bad happens to her? What if I lose her, too?"

"We're going to find her, Fern," Mr. Johnson says. "You'll see. We'll find her."

Part of me is glad that Tinny ran away. I hate

Tinny. I hate her being in my town and stealing the hugs from Fern that should be mine. Maybe Fern's right. I am jealous of Tinny. But so what? I was here first.

Part of me feels like that, but the other part of me can't forget Fern's words.

What if I lose her, too?

Tinny is the only real family Fern has left. Mr. Fern is dead. Her sister is dead, and so is Tinny's mom. Even if she is rotten, maybe Tinny is better than no family at all.

Tinny is a sneak and a thief and a runaway, but she told the truth about the money. And yesterday, she kept the Ring Man from grabbing me and she kept my secret, too. Maybe if I'd done something, she wouldn't have run away. Maybe then, Fern's heart wouldn't be breaking.

What will happen to Fern if she loses one more person she loves with all her heart?

What will happen to Fern if her heart breaks into a million tiny pieces?

I look at the green-and-orange afghan hanging on the back of the rocking chair by the window and I know.

Dad's got no idea how long they'll be gone, so he and Fern take me to the Page sisters' house until they get back. Miss Pearl is off visiting somewhere, but Miss Opal is home. She grabs my hand and pulls me into a rickety chair at the kitchen table.

"Oh, Miss Lily," she says, "what a lovely surprise! Won't Pearl be pleased?"

Dad kisses me on the forehead and he and Fern leave.

Miss Opal goes out to the pantry, and when she comes back with some "Oriole" cookies she's surprised to see me.

"Oh, Sapphy!" she says. "When did you get here?"

I have to help Fern. I have to find Tinny, but I can't do it sitting around eating cookies with Miss Opal. When she goes into the other room, I grab a couple of cookies and sneak out the front door. I don't think she'll miss me.

I don't think she'll remember I was ever here.

Tinny's letter is weird. I don't like the way she calls Olena a "backwater pit." Those are the Ring Man's words. She's just using them to sound tough. And there's something else that bugs me, but I can't figure out what.

I just know that I have to find Tinny.

I walk all around Olena but I don't find any clues. I even look in Fern's bottle house but Tinny's not there. There's nothing inside but a red wagon and the crates of empty Pepsi bottles waiting for the deliveryman to come next week and swap them for full ones.

When I step out of the bottle house, I get a creepy feeling like someone is watching me. It's a shivery feeling like late at night when I read a Nancy Drew book and I can feel the danger she's in. Like it's me in the book instead of Nancy.

I'm about to latch the door when something goes *snap* in the bushes behind the bottle house and I freeze. Then a small gray squirrel hops out and chitters at me. I throw a rock at him and he runs away.

I hate squirrels.

I don't know where else to look, so I go to the cottonwood tree. I sit in the branches instead of the V so I can ambush Tinny like she ambushed me, but she doesn't show up.

The cicadas are so loud up in the tree that I have to cover my ears to stand the noise. I've never heard anything so loud. The buzz is electric and it makes me feel like everything else outside the tree is standing still. Then the cicadas stop singing for just a second, and the spell is broken and that creepy feeling comes back like somebody is watching me.

I climb out of the tree and wander around town some more until I'm hot and sweaty and my shirt sticks to my skin. Finally, I go to the post office.

It's cool inside. Lottie Duncan is there gossiping with Lorene Williams and Harold. They don't stop talking when I come in. They don't even slow down.

I go to the back corner and stare at the floor. It's the coolest spot in the post office, and I can hear what they say without even trying.

Harold is busy sorting letters into the post office boxes. From his side of the counter, they are little cubbyholes, but from the lobby, they are rows of tiny brass doors, each with a number and a keyhole with etched stars around it. They are the only fancy things in Olena, besides the windows at the church.

I think about the folded-up Tootsie Pop wrapper that fell from Tinny's pocket in the store: PO309. It's Fern's P.O. box. The box Tinny opened last night to leave her note. Why did she do that? Why didn't she just leave the note at Fern's house or at the store?

The very first box is number one. I wonder if it belongs to someone important, like the mayor or maybe the principal of the school. I look down the rows of boxes to the very last one. Number 100. I scan the numbers again. There are only 100 boxes in the Olena Post Office. What does PO309 mean?

Just then, Lottie says, "Oh, Harold, do you have the address of the County Water Department? You know that nice surveyor man who was renting that room over my garage? He paid up yesterday morning and left, but I found his work shirt in the room."

The Ring Man left yesterday morning.

He was at the cottonwood tree yesterday evening, and I know what that means.

He spent the whole day waiting to catch Tinny alone. And when he caught her, I was there and got in his way. What if I hadn't been there? What would he have done?

I can't forget his cold, horrible eyes. A criminal's eyes.

Then I do something criminal. I go over to the display stand where Harold keeps all the tax forms and postal service brochures. There's a potted African violet on top of it.

I bump against the stand and knock it over. Tax forms fly into the air and the flowerpot hits the glossy tile floor and busts into a hundred pieces.

"Oh, no, Lily!" Lorene yells. She and Lottie

grab at the flying papers. I hear Lottie say, "Can't Paul do something with that child?" as Harold runs to the back to get a broom. Before he comes out again, I'm outside with the stack of wanted posters stuffed under my shirt.

I duck behind the building and run into Hall's Woods. The woods stretch out to the edge of town where our cornfield starts. I run through the woods squeezing the papers against my body so they won't fly loose. Dry leaves and sticks crack under my feet and branches scrape my legs as I run.

I think I hear footsteps behind me, but my heart pounds so loud, I can't tell for sure, and I don't stop to find out. I run out of the woods and down the cornrows and all the way home before I stop.

When I get to the porch, I stand there with my heart banging in my chest and my sides aching and I try to catch my breath. I look over the knee-high rows of corn, but nobody's there. Nobody's chasing me.

Then I think I see a flash of blue at the edge of Hall's Woods, but I watch for a long time and I don't see it again. I'm imagining things.

11

PETE'S ROOM

I SIT ON MY BED AND PULL OUT THE wanted posters. There are at least fifty of them. I stare at the mug shots of murderers and robbers and counterfeiters. I look carefully at each mug shot before I go to the next one. Some of the posters have artist sketches instead of photos, but I study them, too.

I try to imagine each criminal with a haircut like the Ring Man's and wearing a County Water Department shirt. I go through thirty-seven posters and don't find him. Then I look at the next one. Staring at me from number thirty-eight is a pair of eyes I know, but they're not the Ring Man's eyes—they're Tinny's.

They're Tinny's eyes on the face of a thin, pale man. Below the picture is a description of him.

WANTED

For Armed Robbery
And Conspiracy to
Commit Armed
Robbery

Robert Tinsdale Bridges
Ht. 6 feet 1 inch
Wt. 200 pounds
Last seen: Chicago, Illinois

Believed to be armed and Dangerous. Wanted for a series of armed robberies at Chicago area jewelers and pawnbrokers. With accomplice unknown, suspect stole merchandise and cash valued at $250,000.

Accomplice unknown . . .

He's not unknown to me. He's the Ring Man.

Tinny's dad and the Ring Man are robbers.

But why is the Ring Man looking for Tinny's dad? Did he run off with the loot?

I almost laugh. I can just hear Pete say that.

Bugsy stole the loot from Rocko and he's on the lam from the cops.

Somehow Pete could keep a straight face saying that, but it would crack me up pretty good.

It doesn't crack me up now because of those other words: *armed and dangerous.* I don't know if Tinny's dad is dangerous, but I know the Ring Man is, and he's after Tinny.

I think about the Ring Man's eyes and his calm, cold voice. It gives me the chills to think about him coming back to the store like he said he would. He'd stand by the deli case, clicking his cherry Life Saver on his teeth while he looked at the sandwiches and waited for Tinny to show up. What would he do to Tinny if she showed up? What would he do to Fern if Tinny didn't?

I will never break my promise to Pete, but I have to let Dad and Fern know about the Ring Man and the robberies. I have to do it for Fern.

Just then, I hear a noise downstairs in the kitchen like somebody is down there. Maybe it's Dad. I look out the window, but Dad's truck is gone. If someone is in the kitchen, it isn't him.

I grab the poster and sneak down the steps listening as hard as I can. When I get to the bottom, I stand there a long time, but I don't hear anything but the refrigerator in the kitchen and the clock in the dining room. After a minute, I tiptoe to the kitchen, but it's empty. There's nobody in the house but me.

Another shiver runs down my spine, but I shake it off. I've given myself the creeps thinking about the Ring Man, and now I'm imagining things again.

This is stupid. I open the back door and look out. No one is there. Then I go to the front porch but no one is there, either. I'm alone.

I sit on the porch swing and stare at the mug shot of Tinny's dad. Where is he now? He must be far away if the Ring Man can't find him.

It's getting late and the sun turns red and heavy and starts to sink out of the sky. It slides behind the green fields where the road crosses over the hill. I look into the sunset hoping that I can see Dad's truck coming down the road, but I can't. Then the sun is gone.

It's almost night and Dad is still not home.

I wait on the porch swing a little longer, then I go inside and put the poster on the kitchen table where Dad will find it when he gets home. Then I go upstairs.

I walk down the hall and stop at Dad's room.

His bedroom door is open and the window curtains are back so I can see the moon rising over Hall's Woods.

The moon is fat and yellow and lopsided. It turns the green cornrows into soft gray stripes and pushes back the shadows that creep out of the trees and into the field.

I remember the flash of blue in the trees and a shiver runs over my body. I jerk Dad's bedroom door shut and flip on the hallway light. I stand there for a minute until the shiver goes away. Then I cross the hallway toward Pete's room.

I wish Pete was here. Pete wasn't a detective, but he would know what to do. He'd know how to find Tinny and save Fern. He'd know what to do about the Ring Man and Tinny's dad, too. He never read Nancy Drew books or even the Hardy Boys, but Pete was smart.

Pete would know what to do.

❧

As I pass Pete's room, I slide my hand softly over the white door like I've done a million times since he died, but for the first time, his door swings open. The light from the hallway spills onto the floor and I hold my breath and step inside.

T-shirts and dirty socks and books are scattered over the floor. A pair of overalls hangs over Pete's chair and his bed is a mess. Just like Pete left it.

His walls are covered with posters of Humphrey Bogart and James Cagney and the tough-guy heroes from the movies Pete loved. There are candy wrappers in a big heap by the bed like he'd just spent hours lying in bed eating candy and tossing the wrappers on the floor. I close my eyes and breathe in. I can practically smell the candy.

It feels like Pete just left. It's like Pete could walk back in at any minute. But, of course, he won't. Pete is gone.

Gone where I can't follow.

I feel dizzy and hot. I open the window. A breeze pushes back the curtains and I stand there for a long time and let the wind blow over my face.

Then I sit down on Pete's bed. I feel tired and heavy and I reach for his pillow to prop myself up, but it's gone. It's probably under the bed or in the pile of dirty clothes in the corner. I wad his sheet into a ball and rest my head against it.

Memories of Pete swirl around in my mind. Good memories at first of fishing at Johnson's Pond and Pete running through fields and laughing— always laughing.

Then bad memories.

I try to push them out of my mind by thinking about Tinny's letter. What is it that bugs me about her letter? What did she say at the end?

Tell everybody where I went.

There's only one reason Tinny would say that. I think Tinny wants the Ring Man to follow her back to Chicago. That's why she left the note in Fern's P.O. box. Leaving it in the post office is like putting up a giant billboard in the middle of town or announcing it on a loudspeaker: "HEY, RING MAN! I'M GOING TO CHICAGO! COME AND GET ME!"

Is that what Tinny wants? Is she trying to lure him away from Fern?

There's just one problem. Tinny didn't know that the Ring Man was gone from Lottie's. He wasn't at the post office today, so he couldn't get the message. The Ring Man won't know to look in Chicago.

And even if he gets the message, I wonder if he'll believe it. I'm not even sure I do.

Tinny is sneaky and smart. I don't think she'll go back to Chicago. Tinny is someplace else. I try to think of all the places Tinny might really go, but the crickets keep interrupting and I close my eyes to listen for just a second.

And I fall asleep.

I dream about Pete, but it's different this time.

Pete and I are driving fast down a country road in Mr. Fern's sedan. Something bad's going to happen, but I don't remember what.

Pete drives faster and faster, and I squeeze the handle of the car door as hard as I can and hold my breath. I try to close my eyes, but I can't. I can't stop staring at the road ahead where I know something is waiting for us.

Then I see Dad at the edge of the field on Mr. Johnson's green tractor. He's about to drive in front of us, but suddenly he stops and waves, and we zoom past. I let go of the door handle and let out my breath and start to smile.

Then I see her.

Tinny steps into the road ahead of us. She holds up the end of her long silk scarf and it blows behind her in the breeze.

I try to yell at Pete. I try to make him stop, but I can't make a sound. My voice is gone.

The car engine growls and the sedan speeds up. It races at Tinny, who looks right at us but doesn't move.

I turn to Pete to make him stop, but it's not Pete behind the wheel. It's the Ring Man and when he looks at me, his eyes are cold and hard.

And he laughs.

12

THE BARN

I WAKE UP IN THE DARK.

Where am I?

The moon shines through the window onto a pile of clothes and a pair of dirty sneakers. Pete's sneakers. I'm in Pete's room and it's late. The moon has crossed all the way over the house since I came upstairs.

I've been asleep a long, long time.

Then I remember Tinny and that tight, twisty feeling grabs me again. How could I sleep so long? I run to Pete's window and look down at the driveway. Dad's truck is still gone.

The world is gray and black and shadowy. I look out across the road at Fern's barn in the middle of the cornfield. It's like a huge, black ship floating out there all by itself. Like a ghost ship.

I can see why Pete wanted to sneak out there at night. Those shadows called to him. They thrilled him like those shadowy movies he loved so much.

Pete loved it, but the inky blackness that oozes out of the barn and spreads into the cornfield gives me the shivers.

I reach up to close the window, but then I see something flicker far off in the field. A small white light flashes in the dark, and then it's gone. I watch for a minute, and then I see it again.

I run downstairs and outside to the porch and pull on my sandals. I stare out over the field and wait. Then I see the light again. It's by the barn.

I cross the road and stop at the edge of the field. Something holds me back. It's not right to be there without Pete. I can't go to the barn without him. But I have to.

I have to find Tinny. I have to save Fern.

The smell of the corn and the soft dirt under my feet are the same as a million times before. In my mind, I see Pete's face with that sly look, like he's going to do something sneaky. Like he's going to cheat.

And then the breeze picks up and rustles the corn, and I get this feeling like Pete's there beside me. Like he's next to me getting down low in his Olympic runner pose. And then I hear his voice, "Ready . . . set . . ."

And I run. The long corn leaves scratch my bare legs as I run through the field. I run fast like an Olympic runner; fast like there's a ghost on my heels.

A cloud slips over the moon and the field turns black, but I don't need the moonlight to show me the way to the barn. I run like a million times before.

When I get close to the barn, I stop and catch my breath. Then I slip around the corner as quiet as I can. The side door to Fern's barn is cracked open. And there's a dim light inside.

I pull the door open as quietly as I can, but the hinge squeaks and the light goes out. It's pitch-black inside the barn.

My heart pounds in my chest and I want to turn around and run away, but I can't. Instead, I step inside. The barn smells like hay and dust, and the air is cool and still. It's so familiar, it makes me dizzy.

I take a step and then another. My eyes get used to the dark and I can see black shapes on the ground. There's the dead plough and the busted crates, and there are two big shadows ahead of me. I know they're Mr. Fern's cars.

The convertible is under a tarp and its shadow is a big blob, but the sedan is different. Its shadow is sharp and its edges are smooth.

The sedan is uncovered.

I step closer and I can see the smooth fenders and the hood.

The tight, twisty feeling grabs me so hard I can't breathe. I want to run, but my feet won't turn around. It's like something invisible has me and it drags me toward the sedan.

I step closer and closer until I can touch Mr. Fern's car . . . Pete's car.

Then the moonlight comes back, and it shines through the hayloft window onto the sedan and I see Tinny.

Tinny is slumped against the steering wheel with her face toward me and her black hair tossed back.

Her skin is pale and her eyes are closed and sunk into shadowy circles.

She doesn't move.

And it hits me so hard I almost fall over.

Pete slumped over a steering wheel in the gray moonlight.

Tinny doesn't move.

Fern reaches through the window and shakes Pete over and over and over . . .

My arm rises up and my hand slides through the open car window.

Pete! . . . Wake up! . . . Wake up!

Closer and closer. I reach out to touch Tinny's hair. Black like oil on midnight water.

Fern shakes him again and Pete falls over onto the car seat—his eyes wide open. Then the scream starts in a place deep, deep down. Her insides twist tighter and tighter and squeeze the scream up into the night . . .

Pete!

Tinny's eyes snap wide open.

PETE!

The scream explodes the darkness. It's louder than a million cicadas and it burns my ears and my insides. I push my hands against my ears, but the scream is so loud, I can't block it out . . .

PETE!

The scream twists up and pushes out of me so hard I can't stop it.

I scream and scream and I can't stop it when the Ring Man steps out of the shadows and comes toward me.

I scream and scream and I can't stop it when I see Tinny get out of the sedan and run away.

The Ring Man grabs me and shakes me hard.

"Shut up!" he yells. "Shut up!"

I scream and scream and he wraps both hands around my neck and I feel the cold band of his ring on my skin.

He squeezes harder and harder until the

scream can't push past his hands anymore, and it dies inside me and everything gets fuzzy.

Then I hear the *crack* of wood and the Ring Man's eyes roll back in his head and he lets go of my throat and drops to the ground.

And there is Tinny behind him, holding a piece of crate up in the air like a broken baseball bat.

Tinny drops the wood and grabs my hand, "C'mon, Lily!"

She pulls me out of the barn and into the field. The moon is bright again, and Tinny leads me down rows of long silvery leaves that swish behind us as we run.

At the edge of the field, I look across the road and see two trucks in the driveway, and Dad and Fern and Cyril Johnson are on the porch. They're coming down the steps and when they see us, they run.

"Call the cops!" Tinny yells.

Mr. Johnson goes back to the house, but Fern and Dad keep running toward us.

Dad grabs me up in his arms and squeezes me tight so his face is against mine and it's damp where our cheeks press together.

"Lily!" he says. "Lily! You were gone! I couldn't find you."

His voice sounds so scared.

He puts his hands on my shoulders and holds me back a little so he can look at all of me.

"Are you okay?" he asks and for the first time in two years, I look back at him.

I look into Dad's face and it's worn and tired and sad, and I feel my heart break into a million tiny pieces, and the things I've pushed down deep inside me squeeze up and I can't push them back down again.

"Dad . . ."

My voice is scratchy and weak and my throat hurts, but I say it over and over again, "Dad . . . Dad . . ."

He stares at me like it's a word he's never heard before and he's trying to figure it out. Then he pulls me close again and kisses me and everything I've wanted to tell him for so long—everything I'm afraid to tell him—comes out and I can't stop it.

"It's my fault," I say. "It's my fault Pete died. I shut the door. It was me. I shut the door."

I know Dad will hate me now. I know he has to hate me and I wish I hadn't said the words. I wish I had stopped them.

I want to push my words back into the tight, twisty place where they won't hurt anybody but me.

But I can't.

I look down at the ground and try to be

invisible. The tears run down my face and drip into the darkness.

"Lily," Dad says and his voice is soft and gentle, "look at me."

He lifts my face with his hands so I have to look at him, but I shift my eyes away so I can't see him.

"Look at me," he says again. He says it so softly and gently that I have to look at him.

"It's not your fault," he says and his voice is barely more than a whisper. "You couldn't know about the fumes. You couldn't know, Lily."

He stops and closes his eyes and a wave of pain flows over him. Then he swallows hard, and when he opens his eyes, they're full of tears.

"It's not your fault, Lily," he says. "It's nobody's fault."

Then Dad pulls me close again and presses his cheek against mine.

"Let him go, Lily," he whispers. "Let him go."

13

NOT EVEN DREAMS

EVERYTHING AFTER THAT BLURS together.

Cyril Johnson and Dad running to the barn . . . The police in the field with their long flashlights . . . Fern hugging me close and calling me a Poor Motherless Child . . . The smell of Fresca and barbecue and honeysuckle perfume filling my lungs while I wrap my arms tight around Fern and don't let go for a long, long time . . .

They find the Ring Man crawling through

the corn. They handcuff him and drag him back to the police cars.

He's wearing a blue shirt.

When he sees me and Tinny, he stares at us so hard I have to look away, but Tinny sticks her head up in the air like the Queen of Siam and stares right back at him.

Tinny tells the police how she pretended to run away. She stashed the food and supplies she stole in the trunk of the sedan. She planned to stay in the barn until everyone gave up looking for her. Then she'd head to Mexico or Canada when the coast was clear.

She fooled everybody but the Ring Man. It's hard to fool criminals—even when you act like one. It was the Ring Man I saw in the woods. He was watching me. Hoping I'd lead him to Tinny.

And I guess I did.

I led him on a wild-goose chase all around Olena. Then I led him right back to our house where Tinny was waiting the whole time. She was in Pete's room, because she knew Fern would look in the barn first and find her there. She hid in Pete's room until everyone went off looking for her somewhere else. Then she sneaked to the barn.

It was Tinny I heard in the kitchen. Tinny who ate all the candy in Pete's room and took his pillow.

The Ring Man saw Tinny sneak out of the house and run to Fern's barn. He waited until night to follow her, so nobody would see him. But I saw him.

Finally, the police leave and Mr. Johnson drives Fern and Tinny back home, and it's just me and Dad on the porch. It's almost dawn and the gray and black shadows fade into a soft green haze that floats over the cornrows.

We sit on the porch swing and Dad puts his

arm around me. He hums as we swing back and forth and I lean against him, heavier and heavier, and when I sleep, not even dreams can find me.

I wake up late and we go to Fern's house in the afternoon. A man from the FBI is coming to talk with Tinny. It makes Fern nervous and she wants us to be there, too.

When we get there, Dad goes to the kitchen with Fern and I wait in the parlor. Fern's house is cozy and it smells like honeysuckle perfume. The wallpaper is faded and the furniture is covered with crocheted afghans and there are photographs all over the walls. Long-ago pictures of long-ago people. Fern's people.

Two color photos sit on a table by the window. One is of a man and a woman and a little girl with black hair. The woman has long black hair and a crooked smile, and she looks like Tinny except for her eyes. Around her neck, she wears a long silk scarf, covered in flowers. Tinny's scarf.

I recognize the man. He's much younger than in his mug shot, and he's smiling with his head tossed back. They're happy.

I pick up the other picture. Two girls about my age stand together in front of a lilac bush with their arms around each other. One is Tinny's mom.

"That's my mom and Cyril Johnson's daughter."

I put the picture down and turn around.

Tinny's standing there with her fists crammed down into her pockets. Her hair is tied back with her flowered scarf.

"They're pretty," I whisper.

It's hard to talk. My voice is scratchy and weak and my neck is black and blue where the Ring Man choked me.

Tinny sees the bruises and she gets a terrible look on her face.

"Lily . . ." she says. Her voice sounds sad and worried, and it surprises me.

Tinny always acts so tough, but maybe she isn't really. Maybe she just has to act that way. Tinny is still sneaky, but maybe she's not so mean after all. Maybe she's just a scared twelve-year-old girl without a mom. Like me.

Fern says I saved Tinny. I found her in the barn when no one else could, and I stopped the Ring Man before he could hurt her. Maybe that's true, I don't know. But when I think about the look in Dad's eyes when I said his name, I think that maybe it's *Tinny* who saved *me*.

Tinny takes the scarf out of her hair and wraps it gently around my neck to hide the bruises. She arranges the scarf so the ends dangle over my shoulder. Then she steps back and looks at me.

I smile at her.

"What's the matter?" I whisper. "Ain't you never seen a shark bite?"

The FBI agent knocks on the door and Fern brings him into the parlor. He isn't tall and dark and mysterious like the agents in Pete's old movies.

He's almost bald and kind of pudgy, and his suit doesn't fit him very well. He's serious, but there's something kind about him, too.

He walks up to Tinny.

"Are you Iris Tinsdale Bridges?" he asks.

"We call her Tinny," Fern says.

"Tinny," the agent says softly, "I'm Agent Daniels of the FBI. I need to ask you some questions about your father."

"What about him?" Tinny asks and she pushes her hands deep down into her pockets again.

"We believe your father was involved in some

robberies in Chicago with Jake Hunston, the man the police arrested last night. Do you know where your father is, Tinny?"

"No," she says and she looks hard at her shoes.

"We believe he has a large amount of money from the robberies, and that's what Jake Hunston was after. Do you know anything about that?"

Tinny looks up and takes her hands out of her pockets. She raises her head and looks him square in the eye. She tilts her head back a little. Not like she's the Queen of Siam—but maybe a duchess.

"No, sir," she says. "I don't know anything about any money. My dad put me on a bus in Chicago and gave me ten dollars for food on the trip. That's all I know."

Agent Daniels looks hard at Tinny for a moment. He looks like he wants to ask her another question, but he just says, "Please let us know if you remember anything."

Dad and Fern go outside with him, and Tinny and I are alone in the parlor.

Tinny is lying. I can tell by the way she took her hands out of her pockets and tilted her head back just a tiny bit, and by the way she looked him right in the eye when she answered.

"You have to tell them where the money is," I say.

"I don't know where it is," she says. She tries to sound tough, but it doesn't work.

I know why Tinny's lying and I don't blame her. If they catch her dad, he'll go to jail—and she knows it. But if they don't find the money, Jake will be back, and Tinny knows that, too.

I walk to the table and pick up the picture of Tinny's family.

"They look happy," I say.

Tinny doesn't say anything. She just takes the picture and stares at it. Then she softly touches each person in the picture, like she's counting them to make sure they're still there, and puts the picture on the table.

Tinny pulls a Tootsie Pop out of her pocket and takes off the wrapper. She crams the sucker in her mouth so her cheek bulges out like a chipmunk's. She carefully folds the wrapper over and over into a tiny cube. And that's when I get it.

"You have to tell them," I say and I look hard at Tinny until she looks back at me.

"Tell them what?" she asks.

"Tell them that the money is in a Chicago post office box," I say. "Number three-oh-nine."

Tinny looks surprised, but just for a second, then she gives me a crooked little smile and says, "Well, well. You really are a regular Nancy Drew, aren't you?"

Maybe I do feel like Nancy Drew just a little, but I don't want to. Nancy is kind of spoiled. She drives a fancy car and solves made-up mysteries that don't really matter at all. If I'm right, the police will find the money and they'll find Tinny's dad, too, and then he'll go to jail.

Tinny's smile fades and she looks sad, but maybe a little relieved.

"Dad has a plan," she says. "He'll put the money in a package in his P.O. box in Chicago. He always says the best place to hide something is around lots of people, because that's the last place they look. That's why I hid in your house. Who would look for me there?"

Tinny gives me that crooked smile again.

"Dad will find someplace where Jake can't track him down—maybe Mexico or Canada," she says. "Then, when he's all settled, the post office will forward the package to the new address, and Dad will send for me. He'll do it. It's just going to take a while. That's all."

Tinny says the last part like she's trying to convince herself it's true. I don't think it is, though. I don't think Tinny's dad will send for her. If he really cared about her, he would have given her more of the money so she wouldn't have to steal from Fern. If he really cared, he wouldn't have sent her away in the first place.

I look in Tinny's eyes. I can tell she doesn't believe it, either.

"You have to tell them," I say again. This time, Tinny waits a long time before she answers.

"I know," she says.

14

THE POSTCARD

TINNY TAKES THE THIN RED RIBBON from around her neck, grabs the tiny brass key dangling from it and opens Fern's P.O. box. Then she puts the ribbon back on and tucks the key under her shirt so she won't lose it. Tinny has worn the key around her neck every day since Fern gave it to her and asked her to be in charge of the mail. She even wears it on Sundays when there isn't any mail to check.

I always go with Tinny to the post office. Fern doesn't get much mail, except bills and some crochet magazines. But sometimes she gets the Sears catalog, and Tinny and I take it to the cottonwood tree and sit in the branches and think about all the things we'd buy if we were rich.

Today, there's only one piece of mail in the box. Tinny reaches her hand inside and pulls out a postcard. Her breath catches for just an instant and almost as fast, she sweeps the card into her back pocket and runs out the door.

Tinny runs straight to the cottonwood tree and climbs up extra high and doesn't say a word when I climb up and sit by her.

"What is it?" I ask, but I already know the answer.

I saw the postcard when Tinny pulled it out of the P.O. box. It had a picture of a giant cactus wearing a dorky sombrero and big orange letters saying HOWDY PARTNER! There's only one person who would send Tinny a card like that.

I know that Tinny is dying to look at the card, but

I think maybe she's scared, too, because she doesn't do it. We both sit as still as stone and it feels like the whole world is holding its breath. Finally, Tinny pulls the card out of her pocket and holds it so she can see the cactus but not the writing on the back.

"I don't want to read it," she says.

She starts to put the card away, but then she stops and takes a deep breath and flips it over. There isn't much on the other side. A flag stamp. Tinny's name and Fern's address. And a sloppy handwritten note in blue ink: *I thought you might like this. Just wanted to say "Hi."*

That's all.

Tinny flips the card over and over looking for more. Looking for something. Looking for anything. But there isn't anything to find. The postmark is blurry and she can't even tell where the card came from or when he mailed it.

"I guess he just wanted to say, 'Hi,'" she says

and she glides her hand over the glossy picture and straightens the corner of the card just a bit.

Then Tinny slides the card back into her pocket and we don't say anything, because there's nothing to say and there never will be. Tinny and I won't ever talk about the card again and we won't tell anyone either. Not even Fern.

It'll be our secret—the card where Tinny's dad said, "Goodbye."

We don't look at each other as we sit in the tree and we don't talk, but after a while, Tinny starts to hum. Then she swings her legs back and forth and she says, "Wish I had an orange Push-Up."

And I know it's okay. I know that Tinny's okay.

"Race you to Fern's!" I say.

"Beat you to Fern's!" Tinny says and she laughs.

Tinny scrambles down the cottonwood tree to the lowest branch and jumps to the ground and takes off running. And I'm right behind her.

15

CICADA SUMMER

TINNY CAME TO TOWN WITH THE cicadas. Summer is almost over now and the cicadas are nearly all gone, but Tinny is still here.

The FBI tracked the money from the P.O. box in Chicago, to California, and then again to Oregon. They found most of the money, but not Tinny's dad. He got away. Maybe he's in Mexico or Canada.

Even though Nancy Drew wouldn't approve, I'm glad.

They found the Ring Man's fingerprints on the

money and some people in Chicago identified him, so he won't be getting out of jail for a really, really long time. And when he does get out, I don't think he'll come back to Olena.

Fern gave Dad a cookbook, and I'm helping him learn to use it. We've already made spaghetti. We tried to make lasagna but it was a little too crunchy. Dad says lasagna shouldn't be crunchy, so we have to try it again.

When we get good at cooking, we're going to make dinner for Fern and Miss Pearl and Miss Opal for a change. Until then, we have our Old Lady Parties every Friday night just like we always have, except now Tinny comes along, too.

Tinny and I help Fern in the store during the day when it's too hot to do anything else. Fern gives us ice cream Drumsticks and orange Push-Ups, and we stand in front of the big fan and eat fast before they melt.

Tinny works in the store for one half-hour for every treat that Fern gives her. Fern says she doesn't have to do that, but Tinny says she does. Tinny worked for a whole week to pay for the food she took when she hid in the barn.

I think Tinny wants Fern to know she's not a thief like her father, but she'd never say it. Fern already knows that, and so do I. It takes more than stealing to be a thief.

Once I asked Tinny if she missed her father very much.

She said it was the stupidest question in the whole world and how could anybody ask such a stupid question? And I guess it was, but after a while, she answered it anyway.

She said that she missed him a lot sometimes, but sometimes she didn't too much. She figured it made her a bad person, but sometimes she pretended he was dead just so she could know where he was.

It would be nice to know where he was—even if it was in a graveyard.

We spend a lot of time in the cottonwood tree. We sit up in the branches, because there's not room down in the V for both of us.

I tell Tinny everything I know about Olena. I tell her all about the Reverend Riley White and all the news I get from the store. I tell her about school and the place where I hide Nancy Drew mysteries.

I could talk all day just telling her what I know, but after a while I get quiet and Tinny tells me about Chicago. She tells me about her dad and the things he did up there with people like the Ring Man—creepy men with cold eyes and mug shots.

Pete would love Tinny's stories. He'd make her tell them over and over if he was here. I'd like to hear them over and over, too, but I let Tinny decide what she wants to tell me.

Tinny could help me find the thief who stole

The Haunted Showboat. We could be like a couple of Nancy Drews, if I asked her, but I don't think I will. Nancy Drew is fun, and her books give me the shivers when I'm reading late at night instead of sleeping, but it's not the real thing. It's not real crimes or real bad guys who hurt people like Tinny. People like me.

Tinny's seen too much of the real thing to playact. She's seen too much bad stuff to want to do it for fun, so I don't think I'll ask her.

The cicadas are dying off and their buzz isn't as loud as it was. We find their crispy, brown shells clinging to the branches of the cottonwood. Dad says the cicadas crack open the backs of their shells and crawl out with a new skin that gets hard. Then they mate and they die, but their children crawl down into the ground and wait for their turn to come out into the light. It'll be seventeen years before they come out again.

Seventeen years before we have another Cicada Summer.

I'll be old then, but I hope Tinny will still be here. Fern wants her to stay forever, but Tinny says that maybe she'll go to Mexico or Canada sometime.

Tinny is used to running away. She's used to being on the lookout. She doesn't let anyone sneak up on her and catch her. But maybe if she's not careful, Olena will sneak up on her. Maybe if she's not careful, Fern will sneak up on her and capture her heart. Maybe I will.

Maybe we already have.

Tinny talks about leaving, but I don't think she will. You can tell everything you need to know about a person by looking in their eyes.

And when I look into Tinny's eyes, I know that she's here to stay.

16

DRIVING

I DREAM ABOUT PETE AGAIN.

We're in Mr. Fern's sedan like always, except the air is cool and it's sweet like fresh rain. We splash through new puddles as we drive past the corn. The stalks are tall and the ears are ripe with silk tassels hanging off them.

When we pass trees along the fencerows, the buzz of cicadas fills the car and Pete smiles. Then we drive on and the sound fades, but Pete keeps smiling.

Pete looks ahead at the red sun hanging over

the fields. At the road where it disappears over the hill.

He looks even farther than that.

When we pass Fern's barn, Pete honks and waves.

"Thanks for the car, Mr. Fern!" he yells and then he laughs, and so do I.

It feels so good to sit with Pete and hear the cicadas and smell the wet fields and the corn. I close my eyes and breathe it all in.

Then I hear the engine growl and I feel the car speed up. I open my eyes and see our house up the road. It looks pink where the sunset hits the white siding. Dad's zinnias lean against the porch, red and pink and orange.

It's so beautiful.

The window is open and the lace curtain flaps in the breeze and I can see the rocking chair with Fern's afghan draped over the back.

Pete looks at the house for just a second and then stares straight ahead and grips the wheel hard. He doesn't think I see him glance at me in the rearview mirror, but I do.

He stares at the road ahead and I know what he wants to do. He wants to drive on forever. He wants to keep going down that road where the red sun is melting into the fields.

He wants to keep going and he wants to take me with him.

I want to go, too. I want to drive forever with my beautiful Pete. To watch his eyes change from gray to green with the sky. To see him smile and to hear him laugh.

I look again at the house and I see someone behind the lace curtains. It's Dad. His left hand brushes the faded denim of his overalls pocket feeling for the keys like it has a thousand times today. Just to be sure.

I look at Pete, and this time he looks at me.

"I'm sorry," I whisper.

Pete smiles and stops the car in front of our house. I open the door and slide out, but Pete grabs my wrist.

"See ya around, toots," he says softly and he looks into my eyes and over my face like he's trying to memorize me. He squeezes my wrist just a little and holds it like that for a long time.

Then he lets go and laughs and I close the car door and watch him drive away.

I stand there a long time and watch his car get smaller and smaller until at last it passes over the hill and is gone.

Then I cross the road and brush past the red and pink and orange zinnias to the porch.

And I go home.

ACKNOWLEDGMENTS

I AM GRATEFUL TO SO MANY PEOPLE who helped during the writing of this book. Special thanks to Michael, for everything . . . and everything else, besides. To Barry Goldblatt—super-agent extraordinaire. To Jo Knowles and Laura Ruby, for helping me get a clue when I needed it the most. To Howard, Jason, Valerie, Amalia, Chad, Scott, and the entire Abrams gang for your amazing support. To Lindsay Berenson, Katie Uram, and Andrew Uram for your thoughts and wisdom. And most especially, to my editor, Susan Van Metre, who loves Olena as much as I do, and whose smart, generous guidance and thoughtfulness have made all the difference. And finally, to the Beatys, who forever and for always make Olena my home.

ABOUT THE AUTHOR

ANDREA BEATY WAS RAISED IN A small southern Illinois town, where her family ran a tiny grocery store. When she wasn't roaming nearby fields with her brothers and sisters, she was reading Nancy Drew mysteries up in the branches of a maple tree.

Andrea now lives outside Chicago with her family. She is the author of *When Giants Come to Play*, illustrated by Kevin Hawkes, and *Iggy Peck, Architect*, illustrated by David Roberts. Andrea blogs about funny books for kids at www.ThreeSillyChicks.com. Learn more about her at www.AndreaBeaty.com.

THIS BOOK WAS ART DIRECTED by Chad W. Beckerman. The text is set in 12-point Adobe Caslon, a font designed by Carol Twombly and based on William Caslon's eighteenth-century typefaces. The display type was created by John Hendrix.